PRETEND FOR ME

RIVER LAURENT

Pretend For Me

978-1-911608-31-8

ACKNOWLEDGMENTS

Thank You

Leanore Elliott
Brittany Urbaniak
Michelle Barber

CHAPTER 1

WILLOW

"The most amazing thing happened to me today," Lorraine declared as she burst through the front door of our tiny apartment.

I lowered the book I was reading. "What?"

"You WILL *never* believe what I've got in my hand," she shouted, dancing the rumba, and waving a black card in her hand. Her eyes were shining like two very green buttons.

I looked at her expectantly. Unlike me, Lorraine was an extremely dramatic person. She had what one would call a big personality. She was always the live wire at any party. The one that hit the dance floor first and the last to leave it. She was also my best friend and the only person in the world I trusted.

I was born a heroin baby, no father, no mother, and suffering withdrawal symptoms. It was in my records that a nurse called Miriam sat for hours in front of my incubator stroking me through the holes in the sides. I still wonder about her because after her, I knew no love throughout my childhood.

Just foster families, five to be exact, who took care of me in exchange for money. I guess I have to count myself lucky since I was never beaten or sexually abused. I was just ignored.

I couldn't blame them. I was a mousy, bespectacled, quiet child.

My life had been dull and loveless and the only pleasure I found was from reading. At first, fairy tales and books about child detectives, then when I was thirteen, I read my first romance book. That was it. I was hooked. Within those pages, I slipped into another wonderful world where gorgeous Alpha men saw beauty in ordinary gray girls like me, and fell in love with them. I spent hours and hours absorbed in that delightful fantasy world.

Lorraine had stopped dancing, so I put my book on my lap and gave her my full attention. "What is it?" I asked mildly.

"What is it?" she demanded. "That's your reaction to me saying the most amazing thing has happened to me?"

I hid a smile at her annoyance. "All right. Tell me what is this amazing thing that has happened to you."

She rushed to the sofa and held the card in front of me.

I took it and glanced at it. The card was thick and black and the writing was embossed in gold. It seemed to be an invitation to a party, and I honestly could not for the life of me imagine how it could be classed as amazing.

"Well?" she prompted.

I looked up at her and shrugged. "What is it? It just looks like an invitation to a party to me."

"Just an invitation to a party?" she screeched. "Have you never heard of the Ambonnay Gala?"

I shook my head. "No. Should I have?"

She sank down next to me. "Guuuurl, it is time you got your cute little button nose out of those romance books of yours and live a little. The Ambonnay Gala is just the most important party in the world. I mean, people kill to go to these events."

I made a disbelieving face.

"I'm serious. This party is where the crème de la crème of society go. It is packed with the 0.1 percent. Last year, Kim Kardashian tried to go. She hinted about it on Twitter, but in the end she couldn't get an invite, so she had to pretend she didn't want to go because she was too busy bickering with her mother, one of her sisters, husband, or kids."

I gave the card back to her. "Right. So how did you get your hot paws on this then?"

"That is the second most amazing part of my story. It was purely by chance. It could so easily have gone to someone else."

I smiled and sat back in anticipation of a good story.

She gave me a grin and put the card on the table. "Bella was sick today, so Matthew asked me to take over her section. At about eight, a couple came in. The woman was one of those Hollywood actress types. She was wearing a divine red dress and her face was so done up you couldn't tell if she was in her late twenties or seventies. The guy though, was very handsome and young, maybe in his early twenties. I got the impression he was subservient to her, like he was her body-

3

guard or masseur. Even so, they made a good-looking couple so I showed them to table nine."

I nodded. That's what I would have done too, if I had been working in the restaurant tonight. Table nine was where we put the beautiful people because it was right in the middle and everybody got to see them. It made the restaurant look glamorous.

"The whole time they kept holding hands and looking deep into each other's eyes. They were so madly in love the woman hardly touched her meal. Then over dessert, the man gets on his knees in front of the whole restaurant and proposes to her."

My eyebrows rose in surprise. All the time I'd been working in that restaurant nothing like this had ever happened.

"She was so happy she cried. Well, she didn't really cry, but she dabbed away some imaginary tears from her perfectly made-up eyes. She paid the bill, and when I brought her receipt back, she gave me this invitation. She said she was leaving her husband so she no longer needed it. I mean, can you believe it? I was just at the right place at the right time."

I frowned. "So you're going to go to this party?"

"*We* are," she stated with a grin.

CHAPTER 2

WILLOW

"**N**o, no, no," I said shaking my head vigorously. "Count me out."

"Oh, come on, Willow, it's going to be so fun!"

"Yeah, I really don't think that it's my kind of thing."

"What are the chances that we would get an invite to something like this?" she pointed out eagerly. "I mean, of all the people in the world she could have given that invite to, she gave it to me. That means we have to go, doesn't it? It's fate! It's kismet! It's a chance to buy fancy dresses and drink champagne for the evening!"

The way she was selling it, I knew that I should just concede and accept her invitation to an adventure unlike anything I'd ever known before. Then for her, a rambunctious ball of energy that sparked to life every time she walked into a room... Hell, she would set the world on fire if she got the chance... while I stood on the nerdier end of the spectrum.

"I'd be like a fish out of water in that kind of environment."

"Oh no, you wouldn't. Just leave it to me. I'll take care of everything. I'll be your fairy godmother. I'll make you look so beautiful you'll be like Cinderella at the ball. It'll be a chance to see how those kinds of people live." She hugged one of the couch cushions while widening her eyes at me pleadingly.

"Listen Lorraine. I know you mean well and you think you're doing me a favor by taking me to this party, but I really don't want to go. Why don't you take Susan or even Bella? They would love it," I argued, although I got the feeling any argument on my part would be thoroughly steamrollered. When she got an idea into her head, it was impossible to shift it, and this one seemed like it had taken a very particular hold in her brain.

"But I want you to go with me."

"I would be so awkward around all those celebrities and billionaires."

"No, you won't. You'll be with me. I promise I won't let you out of my sight. Come on, it will be such a great experience. It'll be something to tell our grandchildren."

I shook my head. "Thanks, but no thanks."

She sat back and stared at me. "Remember that time when you came down with the female version of man flu?"

"I had pneumonia," I corrected dryly.

She waved her hand carelessly to show she had no interest in petty details. "I covered five shifts for you, which means I didn't have a break for two whole weeks. When I said I didn't want you to pay me back, you said you would owe me one. Well, I'm calling in the favor now.

I gazed into her serious eyes. She really wanted me to go with her. Thoughts about our lives together flashed into my brain. How hard we worked just to cover our bills. Both of us working every shift and Lorraine worked as a housecleaner in a swanky apartment two mornings a week. At least, I had my books to hide in. She had nothing. We were both orphans. This was Lorraine, my best friend. The person I cared about most in the whole world and I'd do everything in my power to make her happy. Going to a party where I would feel awkward and self-conscious all night would be nothing if it would make her happy.

I smiled at her. "Of course, I'll go with you. We'll be like two Cinderellas at the ball."

As if she had been stung in the butt, she leaped into the air with a scream. Pulling me up by my wrists and laughing madly, she dragged me along as she energetically did her happy dance. "I got a good feeling about this. I promise, you won't regret saying yes," she gasped.

I probably would, but what the hell. If it made her happy, I was good with it.

"Right. First thing we're going to need are some gorgeous designer outfits," Lorraine said, giddy with excitement.

"Hang on, I'm not dropping big money on this night," I warned her. "I don't care if it is how the other half lives. I've got rent to pay at the end of the month."

"Oh, we'll just make it look like we dropped a big pile of money," she assured me. "We won't actually pay that much. We'll have to buy new shoes, of course, but other than that, we won't need to spend any money. I have a friend who works at a salon not far from here. I'm sure she could squeeze us in for some updos, and you know the place where I clean."

I nodded. She cleans for a woman called Beverley, who lives on her own in a penthouse suite. The youngest daughter of a billionaire, she's forever jetting off to parties all over the world.

"Beverley's gone on vacation," Lorraine said. "But she once said if I really needed to borrow a dress for a special event I could look through her collection. Since you and I are more or less the same size…"

And just like that, I was swept along on her crazy adventure. I knew I was getting wrapped up in something I didn't necessarily want to be entangled in. I also knew I had no choice in the matter either way. Once Lorraine set her mind to something, she would not be swayed from it, no matter what. She could usually convince me that whatever she was up to was a good idea for me, too. Apart from her taste in men. That, she would never get me on side with.

Though perhaps I didn't have much room to talk when it came to dating, given that I had been pretty much static in my singleness for the last couple of years. There had been a few half-hearted dates here and there, but nothing that I could actually see going anywhere. No one who seriously did anything for me and it was clear they weren't too interested in what I had to offer either. Which I supposed was fine, but I was starting to wonder if I needed to assume more of Lorraine's attitude to get a guy; be out-there, bold, big and brash. Problem was-I wasn't sure how long I could pull that off before they saw straight through me.

"Okay, I think these shoes will work," Lorraine declared with certainty once she had pretty much turned the contents of the bottom shelf of my wardrobe out onto the floor of my bedroom.

"Oh no, those hurt my toes."

"No pain no gain. You have to suffer a little for beauty," she replied loftily. "Do you have make-up? We need to come up with something glamorous for you. You need to look like you could have come off the red carpet..."

"Good luck with that," I scoffed doubtfully.

Then Lorraine got that look on her face as if she knew something I didn't.

CHAPTER 3

WILLOW

I t had been months since I'd been out to a party, let alone one that was meant to be as crazy-exclusive as this one. So yes, there was a growing excitement in my belly, but more than that, there was nervousness that they would take one look at me and laugh me out of the damn place. Which I wouldn't have blamed them for.

As we walked the pavement on our way to Beverley's apartment, I listened quietly as Lorraine ran a monologue about what we would wear, how we were going to present ourselves, and what we would to do once we arrived there.

I felt like a total fraud. Dressing up in borrowed plumes and pretending to be something I wasn't.

****

"ow," I breathed out as the elevator doors opened and we stood in a space that looked as if it was made of mostly glass.

"It's gorgeous, isn't it?"

I walked to a window and looked out over the breathtaking view. "Hell, Lor, you must spend all your time cleaning these windows. Look at them. They're all so massive and there's so many of them."

"Come on," she says briskly. "Let's get you a dress."

I turned away from the window. "Are you sure about this? She said *you* could borrow something but she didn't say anything about me using anything of hers."

"Don't be such a downer. She won't care. Wait till you see her wardrobe. It's bigger than our apartment and most of the time she only wears her clothes once then she sells them to this woman who has a shop downtown for second-hand designer gear. Anyway, we'll have everything professionally cleaned and back in their place faster than you can say Aladdin."

I followed her into a massive all white bedroom. "Wow, how wonderful to be able to live like this."

Lorraine threw open a door and I walked into the biggest walk-in wardrobe, I'd ever seen. I could have happily lived in this space.

Lorraine didn't waste any time as she moved to one wall and slid all the doors open. Not only were the rails full of clothes, a lot of them still had their tags on them. She turned to me, a wide grin on her face. "Take your pick, Cinderella."

11

I moved forward gingerly. "What if I spill my drink on the dress or something?"

She rolled her eyes dramatically. "It's called professional cleaning for a reason. Now stop wasting time. We've got appointments at the hairdresser in an hour. You have thirty minutes to pick a dress."

"What are you going to wear?"

Her eyes lit up. "I know exactly what I'm wearing." She went to the end of the rack, pulled out a criminally sexy red dress with a seductive slit up the side, and held it under her chin. "This is my ball gown."

"Whoa! It's really beautiful, Lor. There won't be a red-blooded man at that party who won't want to tear it off you with his teeth."

"I know," she agreed without the least trace of fake modesty. "Now you."

I turned to stare undecidedly at the long row of clothes. Really, it was almost impossible for me to try and chose something. Everything was so divine. So not me.

Lorraine walked past me and pulled out a black velvet dress. "This is what I think would look great on you. You don't have to choose it of course, but…"

What was there not to like about the black velvet number she held up? It had a sweetheart neckline and was beautifully cut to hug a woman's curves without jamming them in the face of anyone wandering by.

"Go on. Try it on."

I took the dress from her. "Aren't you going to try the green one too?"

She raised her eyebrows at me. "Do I look like someone who hasn't already put on that dress three hundred times?"

I laughed and started unbuttoning my jeans. I pulled the dress carefully over my hips and turned around so Lorraine could zip me up.

"Done. Let's see what you look like then."

I turned around.

"OMG! It's perfect," she announced triumphantly, clapping her hand to her mouth.

I glanced in the mirror and stared at my reflection in shock. She was right. The dress was a dream and I could already see how perfectly it would go with the painful shoes Lorraine had already picked out for me.

She took me to the accessories drawers then we both chose some necklaces and bracelets to go with our respective dresses then we headed out.

I was starting to get just a little excited about what the night had in store for me. There was no harm in just sitting back and seeing what happened, right?

"Okay, next stop hairdresser," Lorraine announced, linking her arm through mine.

I couldn't help but smile at her. She kept life so exciting. I wasn't sure what I would do without her. Probably a whole lot of sitting around at home, reading and drinking too much wine. "So who is this hairdresser then?"

"Gary is just this gay guy I met at the laundromat," she explained.

I frowned. "Laundromat?"

"Yeah, remember that time our washing machine broke. Anyway, we got on like a house on fire and he told me he works in a high-end salon, so if I ever needed to get done up for an event or something he would fit me in."

"Are you sure he'll be all right with me tagging along?"

"You don't have to worry. He's going to fit you in. Stylists probably can't wait to get their hands on your type of hair. Its virgin hair, isn't it?"

I patted the thick bun I had tossed my hair up into. True, this would be the first time I visited a salon in a year or so. I probably should make the effort to get in a little more frequently. My hair was dark brown, lush and one of my favorite things about myself. I loved the way it looked and felt, even if I hadn't had it styled, shaped or colored. Maybe even because of that. There wasn't a lot that I let flow wild and free about myself, but my hair was one thing I allowed to be natural and loose. As long as my locks were tumbling down my back, I could deal with keeping the rest of my life in careful check.

Lorraine took us to the salon and sure enough, Gary was able to find us both some spare seats and some helper stylists to wash our hair.

"You know, we should probably come up with personas for ourselves," Lorraine remarked from the chair next to mine as the stylists massaged our heads.

"What do you mean?" I asked. "Sounds like we're just making things more complicated than they need to be."

"I mean, we can't just turn up and say that we got the invitation from a lady at a restaurant who gave it to us in lieu of a tip," she pointed out. "We want to come up with something cool. Something that sounds impressive."

"What, like a princess of a made-up country?" I joked.

"Tempting," she conceded. "But no. I think we should aim for something that's a little more believable."

"Like?"

"Maybe CEOs? Could be fun, right? We could come up with the kind of company that we run and everything..."

"I guess we might as well get into this all the way," I admitted, as I felt a shiver run down my spine. I knew this was crazy, one of the craziest things I'd done in a while, but Lorraine made it all sound so plausible, so doable. Almost as if it could be fun!

"Alright, so what's your name going to be?" she asked.

I looked at myself in the mirror, as the stylist massaged my scalp. "Roberta," I replied.

"I like that." Lorraine nodded. "I think I'm going to go with Sophie. Sounds classy, right? Like it could be European or something..."

At this point, both the women washing our hair interrupted us simultaneously and wanted to know exactly what we were up to. Lorraine told them and together with their input, it was decided that we should pretend to be the heads of a publishing company. Lorraine thought I'd read enough books to be convincing. She–wait, no, *Sophie*–would be the CEO of a secretive PR company that celebrities went to whenever they were embroiled in a scandal and needed another coat of whitewash on their reputations.

Once our hair was washed, we were taken to different stations to have our hair cut and blow dried. Barry did Lorraine and a woman in her forties who had her lips set in a hard line approached me, but she lit up when she pulled the towel from my head and my hair cascaded down my back.

"Oh, my goodness," she exclaimed with a laugh, running her fingers through the wet strands. "There's so much to play with here. I understand you're going to a big party tonight. What sort of style were you looking for?"

"I don't really know anything about hair," I confessed. "So just do whatever you want, I don't mind."

"Sure thing," she replied, and began snipping. She trimmed the sides aggressively, but retained a lot of the length at the back. Once she switched off the hairdryer, she began to style my hair. "Alright, you're all done," she announced.

I turned my head from side to side and was surprised at how cool my reflection looked. She had plaited the front of it and let the back fall down over my shoulders in long, carefully-cultivated waves. "It's amazing," I blurted out. "Thank you, seriously. I could never have done this myself..."

"You're welcome. I hope you girls have an amazing time tonight."

Of course, Lorraine looked like a Princess with her lovely blonde hair pulled up on the sides and allowed to flow down to her shoulders.

The two of us headed back to the apartment to finish getting ready. Since Lorraine had made our transformation possible, I agreed to spring for a limousine so we could arrive in style. Lorraine clapped her hands together. "Oh, this is going to be so much fun!"

After we applied makeup, we got changed into our gorgeous outfits.

"Okay, but you look fantastic," Lorraine gasped as soon as she laid eyes on me. "You should dress like this more often. You look like a movie star."

"Yeah, and since I have so many red-carpet premieres to go to... but you look like a million dollars," I said sincerely, gesturing to her whole look.

"Thanks," she replied, checking herself out in the mirror one last time. "You think that the limo's going to be out there by now?"

"I think we should go down and check," I replied, feeling slightly nervous all of a sudden. I turned to her. "Hey, have you got the invitation? I don't want to get turned away after we put all this effort in."

"I've got it." She held up the card and waved it at me.

Then the two of us, hardly able to believe that we were actually doing this, headed to the door and out to the party of a lifetime.

At that moment though, I had no idea just how much the evening would change my life.

CHAPTER 4

I still couldn't fucking believe it. After all this time, after all the effort, and apparently, I still hadn't done enough for him to give me what was due to me.

From the moment I stepped into the lawyer's office, I knew it was going to be bad news. The look on the guy's face told me that. His expression was something between shock and bemusement, as if he himself couldn't believe what he was about to tell me. But I never for one moment thought he would do something like this. If you had told me it would end up being like this, I would have laughed in your face and called you crazy.

And yet…here I was.

My whole life, well, from the time I was seventeen years old, I put all my energy into the family business. When I came into the distribution company that my grandfather, Nathan Grayson started when he was a young man, it was worth at most a million, nothing overly impressive based on what the rest of the industry was pulling in. But I had seen how I could grow the company and seen all the new ways I could breathe more life into it.

"You kids are all the same. You think money grows on trees. Go ahead and try, my hot-blooded boy," my grandfather had said, dismissively. *"But I don't think you're going to get it any further than I already have."*

"We'll see," I had replied, and I knew at that moment I would prove myself to him and anyone else who happened to be paying attention.

Skipping out on college, I taught myself business on the job, learning the ins and outs of the industry through hands-on work at his company. My grandfather ran a tight ship and often, we were short-staffed. I did everything I could. Nothing was too lowly for me. At that time, we only had a small fleet of trucks so whenever we didn't have enough drivers to go around, I'd drive the trucks full of local produce to the fancy hipster places that prided themselves on selling local ingredients.

I started making contacts and friends. One of my new contacts was a banker. I knew we needed to be bigger so I approached him with my business plan.

Soon, we had built a reputation, first in Chicago, then in the state, and then across the whole country. I had proved to myself and anyone else paying attention that I could do anything I set my mind to.

I shifted from driving trucks to working at the office to sign up new clients and field media requests; Grayson Distribution changed the face of the food industry,' according to a few profiles I had managed to rustle up about our business. People were talking about us.

People had heard of us. And we were only just getting started.

By this time, my grandfather had been only too happy to step aside and let me take complete control. He sat back and got a front seat view of how far I took the humble company he had built up.

I knew where the real big money was. I took a gamble. I invested everything and entered the cutthroat world of shipping. The rest, as they say, was history.

For the last twenty years, I had been running the company, but he had never signed over official ownership of the company to me, which had been something of a sore point in our relationship for the last ten years. It was frustrating to know I was running an empire I had built but it wasn't officially mine.

I couldn't understand why he wouldn't let me buy him out, but he always said I would get it when he kicked the bucket. Then I would understand everything when I read his will.

"I'm just worried that you're putting too much of your life into this place, Gabe. I want you to have a wife and kids. When am I going to have some grandkids from you," he once remarked.

I had shaken my head with irritation. *"There is still plenty of time to start a family."*

"I'm saying, you need to take a step back and focus on the most important things for a change. When you're as old as I am, you will realize nothing is more important than family. You won't lie on your deathbed thinking I wish I spent more time in the office," he'd replied.

"Granddad, I'm thirty. I'll start a family when I find the right woman."

"You never go anywhere. How are you going to find a woman?"

"Now is not the right time. I want to grow the company. I want Grayson Incorporated to be the biggest player in the world."

"You should take time off from the business, blow off steam, and have fun. Look at Austin. He is five years younger than you, but he has a good balance going on."

"I'm not sure I would call it a balance," I'd muttered. Austin was my cousin, my uncle's son, and occasionally, he would make some noise about working at the business with me, but he never actually meant it. He was a slacker, a good-time kid first and foremost, but I didn't want to hurt my grandfather's feeling.

My grandfather didn't understand that I didn't want to go out and have fun. My fun was sitting on top of the billion-dollar company that I had built up with my blood, sweat, and tears.

When my grandfather passed away a week ago, I'd been more devastated at his loss than I had thought I would. In a way, the old man and I shared something that no one else did. A deep love for Grayson Inc. For almost all my adult life, I had worked in the shadow of what he'd created and I felt the only way I would be able to honor his legacy was if I threw myself into making his company as great as I could.

When I went to the reading of the will, I was prepared to take full ownership of the company, relieved it would finally be mine, determined that the Grayson name lived on through his company.

But turned out, taking ownership of his company wasn't what he'd had in mind for me at all.

Instead, my grandfather had put a strange stipulation in his will. In order to gain ownership of the business, I not only had to marry, but produce an heir within a year of the date of the will. *Within a year!* I knew this was his way of trying to ensure that I settled down and got my life together the way he wanted me to, but I was still pissed as hell.

In the event I could not produce an heir before the count-down period, the controlling share of the company I had busted my gut to build over the last sixteen years would be simply handed over to Austin. That was just salt in the wound to me—it was just unthinkable. Even the thought of it burned my insides because I knew that little slacker hated my guts and would love the chance to oppose my decisions and rub it in every chance he got.

I had dedicated pretty much my entire adulthood to Grayson Inc. but now it was on the brink of being ripped away from me because I hadn't bothered to knock anyone up on the side? I didn't want my grief at my grandfather's loss all wrapped up in anger at what he had done, but...

How dare he try to run my life from the grave!

****

A s I stalked into the party that evening, I was like a bear with a sore head. I didn't even know why I had come. I never attended such events, but I just knew I couldn't stay in the office or go back home to my empty apartment, all twisted up inside with rage.

I needed to know the world outside me was still turning.

Yeah, my grandfather thought he knew what was best for me, but he didn't have the right to make such an important decision for me. How the hell was I supposed to find a suitable woman, fall in love, and have a kid all inside a year?

Three hundred and sixty-five days was just not enough.

"Hey," a voice purred.

I glanced up, still scowling, to see the kind of woman I normally took to bed. Full lips, big eyes, tight dress, drink in her hand.

"Gabe Grayson," she whispered huskily, while her beautiful blue eyes roved over my face. For all their beauty, there was something cold and hard about those eyes.

And it reminded me again, why I never came to these events. Whenever I did, I inevitably found myself chased around the whole night by gold-diggers hoping they could get claws around my wallet. It was enough to bring me out in a rash.

"Excuse me," I muttered, brushing past her.

The room was packed with kingmakers, most of whom I knew: the Davos crowd, old money, a smattering of European and Middle-Eastern royalty, a couple of grinning politicians and of course, the obligatory swarm of high-class

23

prostitutes. The charity the event was supposedly raising money for was dedicated to the improvement of schools in the area... one of the charitable organizations we had partnered with a long time ago.

Partly, because it was good press, but also partly... because I actually wanted to give back.

Today, I couldn't think about anything other than how I could outmaneuver the bullshit stipulations in my grandfather's will. I was paying my lawyer to work day and night to look for any loopholes we could use. There had to be a way around it, and I'd be damned if I couldn't—

And that was when I saw her.

Tall, with long, dark hair that had been plaited and flowed down her back in a richly lustrous braid. She was wearing a clingy black dress that accentuated every inch of her curvy figure. Yeah, she was beautiful and her dress was so flawlessly simple it had be very expensive, but there was something else different about her.

She stood out.

I could tell instantly she wasn't one of the army of prostitutes, but I knew she didn't belong to the jet set around her either. I couldn't take my eyes off her as I approached the bar at the other end of the room and ordered myself a scotch on the rocks. He pushed me a triple. She hadn't noticed me yet, so I took my time checking her out.

She was sticking close by the side of a woman in a red dress who, like she, didn't belong either. She seemed to be chatting up one of the bartenders. The dark-haired beauty was clutching her glass of wine like it was a life-raft keeping her afloat, while her eyes slid around the room. Whenever they stumbled across someone famous, she bit her lip, as if she was trying to figure out who they were or where she knew them from.

I took a sip of my drink. Whoever she was, she was nice eye-candy. Very nice.

It made me glad I came out tonight. Watching her made me feel a lot calmer than I'd felt in a long time. There was something peaceful about her. The more I watched her the more intrigued I became. I realized she knew she didn't belong, but she liked the freedom it brought her.

The scotch was good and already it was starting to mellow me out as I waited for her eyes to rove around and finally land on me.

And then, the idea hit me. I wouldn't wait for her to notice me. I was going on the prowl myself.

CHAPTER 5

WILLOW

"**E**vening."

As soon as I heard that voice—deep and as smooth as warm chocolate on naked skin—drawling just behind me, I felt something in my stomach curl up with excitement. I knew even before I turned that I was in trouble. His after-shave hit my nostrils. Masculine and smoky. It made the hairs at the back of my neck stand. I wanted to bury my face into his neck and inhale it, commit it to memory.

"Why hello," Lorraine replied instantly, fluttering her lashes at him.

Of course, he would be more interested in her; pretty much every guy we had ever met showed more interest in her blonde good looks.

I took my time. I guess I was putting off the inevitable moment when I locked eyes with the owner of that voice.

Wiping my eyes of all expression, I turned.

He was tall, at least a good few inches taller than me in the torture instruments masquerading as my shoes. Wearing an impeccably cut navy suit that looked as if it must have cost the earth itself and he was goddamn beautiful. His dark hair looked thick and glossy, his jaw was hard and chiseled… his eyes were bottle-green and fringed by impossibly long and luxurious lashes.

He was eyeing us both with interest. Lorraine had been playing it so cool. Well, I didn't want to be the one who was going to make a fool of the both of us. I did my best to play it cool, but I wasn't doing a very good job when I opened my mouth to say hello and nothing came out.

"Grayson, Gabe Grayson," he introduced himself.

The name was vaguely familiar, but I couldn't remember why. Was he some sort of famous model or actor? Lorraine always kept up with celebrity news and I wondered if she knew who he was. I glanced at her and she looked a bit in awe herself.

"Sophie Hudson and Roberta Allen," Lorraine said, waving her hand first at herself, then in my direction.

"I don't think I've seen either of you here before," he remarked, his tone deliberately casual.

I felt a rush of nerves running over me. Had he figured out our game? Do these people have antennae that alert them to outsiders crashing their spaces? He looked completely at ease in this place— the direct opposite of me, in fact.

Luckily, Lorraine tossed her hair over her shoulder and airily announced, "We only recently became beneficiaries of this charity," she replied.

His eyebrows rose.

"Or, uh, benefactors. I forget what the right word is." She grinned.

"Depends if you're donating or receiving," he quipped smoothly, raising his glass to his lips and taking a sip.

His voice was doing things to me. I couldn't even look him in the eyes.

"Ha, ha." Lorraine pretended to chuckle, but her cheeks were a bit pink. She musthave known he was already lost to her.

His eyes slid over to me.

My hands had become clammy with sweat and I could hear my heart pounding in my chest. I didn't want anyone to talk to me. Especially not him. I was happier when I was sitting down, just watching everyone else.

"And what do you do?" he asked. There was no doubt that the question was aimed at me and me alone. He had a nice mouth; soft, full lips, if they were taken separately, no one would have said they belonged on his strong, masculine face, but they were perfect.

"Uh…" I glanced at Lorraine who widened her eyes as if to say, go on, go for it. "Uh, I—um… run a publishing house," I replied, tossing my hair the way Lorraine had done in the hope of claiming some of her confidence. It didn't work. My braid swung around and hit me in the face. I could feel my cheeks burn with embarrassment.

He didn't even blink an eyelid. A confidence came off him in waves, like he knew he owned this place and didn't care who else knew it. "Oh, yeah? What kind of books do you publish?"

"Mostly romance," I replied, surprisingly myself at ease I felt with this subject. "Some erotica."

"Sounds stimulating," he murmured softly.

I wasn't sure what to make of him; couldn't figure out if he was playing with me or if he was serious.

"You mind if I borrow your friend for a dance?" he asked Lorraine, as he extended a hand towards me.

No way this could be real. No way did the hottest guy in this room just walk up to me and ask me to dance with him. I looked over at Lorraine, half-expecting her to say no because we made a pact in the limo on the way here to stay together and not allow ourselves to get separated no matter what.

"Not at all," Lorraine shot back, grinning at me and waving her hands in a shooing motion in my direction. "Go on, go and have fun. I'll be waiting right here when you get back."

Try as I might, I couldn't shake the feeling that this was some kind of joke at my expense. I turned back to Gabe Grayson and reached out for his hand, but as soon as our skin touched, I felt an explosion of shivers coursing down my spine. I nearly pulled back in shock. This was more than I could wrap my head around.

I could feel the eyes of other women staring at him. He was so handsome, so impressive... I had swallowed the hard lump in my throat.

As we approached the dance floor, the band, as if in some prearranged plan by invisible powers that ruled the universe, switched things over to a smoother, slower number. He pulled me in close so that I was pressed against his body. His hands were on my waist as he moved us slowly around the dance floor. I felt as if I was floating, as though the rest of the dancers had faded away around us, and it was just the two of us sweeping around the room a few inches off the floor.

"So," he murmured in my ear, as other dancers surrounded us on the floor. "Something tells me you don't make a habit of coming to events like this."

"Not really," I confessed. "We— we— uh, just became a part of the charity, so I guess that's a—"

"No, I mean," he cut me off. "You don't seem like you come to these kinds of events at all. This is your first one, right?"

I paused for a moment, pulling back and looking at him, and I knew my silence must have given away the truth without me even telling it. Wincing, I decided that I might as well just come and tell him. "No," I confessed. "Both Lorraine and I are waitresses and a woman at the restaurant gave Lorraine the tickets to this place as her tip. Lorraine felt like we should come down here to have a good time, see how the other half lives, I guess."

"So, no publishing company, then?"

I shook my head decisively. "Nope."

"Pity. I was going to ask you about the Fifty Shades thing," he teased.

I smiled, beginning to relax now that I didn't have to keep the game face on. "You can still ask me. I read erotica, so I know a thing or two about it."

He laughed, the sound rich and delicious. "I'll bet you do."

"By the way, I'm Willow and my friend is Lorraine."

He smiled. "Willow suits you much better."

"Tell me, how did you know that we were faking it? I thought we were doing a pretty good job."

"I knew the moment I saw you that you didn't belong here."

I stared up at him dismayed. All the excitement inside me shriveled up. I hated the idea that he saw right through us. Did everyone else know too? Did we look really foolish? "Is that why you came over? To mock us?" I demanded, hurt to my core.

He frowned. "Whoa, not so fast. When I said you didn't belong here, it was a compliment. Look around you. This club is populated by men with one foot in the grave; their spoilt, playboy sons; their wives, or their whores. You don't fit in any of those categories, do you?"

I stared at him. "So why did you come over?"

"I came because I have a proposition for you.

CHAPTER 6

WILLOW

"Hey, buy a girl a drink first," I protested weakly, even though there was nothing to protest against. If he'd straight-up asked me to leave with him, head back to his apartment, and spend the whole night hooking up, I'd have done it.

Maybe it was the couple of glasses of champagne Lorraine and I had in the limo or maybe it was just the piercing green of his eyes, but I didn't have it in me to say no. Or know if I even wanted to. After all, when was the last time someone as gorgeous as he even looked twice at me?

Never was the straight answer.

"Uh… it's not exactly *that* I need you for. This is going to sound completely crazy," he continued, his voice low and caressing. "But I think you can help me out."

"In what way?" I asked, furrowing my brow at him. I couldn't see anything I had that a man like him could possibly need.

"Well, my grandfather started Grayson Incorporated when

he was younger, but I'm the one who turned it from the fledgling business into the billion-dollar concern it is today. I've worked my ass off for years to get it there and make sure it stays there."

"Well, good for you," I replied, not quite sure where he was going with this.

"The problem was my grandfather would never sign over the business to me. He had always said I had to wait for his will to inherit the business," he continued, a tightness in his jaw tipping me off to his intense irritation. "He passed away last week and I was sure it was going to be mine..."

"But?"

"But it turns out that he has some stipulations in place," he replied, lowering his voice. "I have to marry and produce an heir in the next year, or else he's going to hand the business I busted my guts to make successful to my deadbeat cousin."

"Holy shit," I muttered. "That's crazy. Why does your grandfather even want that for you?" I demanded. "It doesn't make sense. If the business is successful—"

"He was worried I was becoming a workaholic and losing sight of the really important stuff in life," he explained. "I guess he had a point, even if I think he's overstating how important the rest of that stuff is."

"Um... why are you telling me this?"

"Do you like being a waitress?'

"The money is useful, but I suck at my job, so there's that."

He laughed.

I grinned. Something about being in this place with him made me feel far removed from the grim reality of my day-to-day life. Here, there was no rent to pay, no bills due, no worries about Leo screaming from the kitchen that I'd screwed up an order.

Gabe stopped laughing abruptly. "I need someone to marry me."

"Well, that shouldn't be too diff—" I began, but then I saw something in his eyes and realized what he was asking. I jerked back with astonishment. "Wait—are you asking me to...?"

"I know it sounds crazy. Trust me, I get it, I do… but it doesn't have to be for long. Less than a year. Just until the rights to the business are signed over."

"Why me?" I croaked.

"Because I looked across the room and saw you," he stated simply.

"You are right. This is crazy," I said shakily.

"Come on," he mocked. "You got dressed up and pretended to be someone else just for fun."

"Yeah, and you saw right through me. So that's how good an actress I am."

"Even the best actress would have failed, because this is a tightly-knit club of insiders. You can't gatecrash it."

"Anyway, we came out for a night of fun. You're asking me to pretend for a year and oh- and there's no way in hell that I'm getting knocked up by you and giving up my own baby. What sort of woman do you think I am?" I huffed furiously.

"I'm not asking you to do that," he replied calmly. "I'll get a surrogate to take care of that. You will have to wear one of those fake pregnancy bumps for a few months when you are out in public though."

"Why would I do that?" I demanded. "Because it sounds like I'm doing you a hell of a favor without too much in return!"

"A million dollars," he replied.

"What?" I gasped. My throat felt like I'd just swallowed a ten-pound cherry.

"I'll give you a million dollars to be my wife for a year."

My jaw dropped.

For a second, we stared at each other. He didn't say anything else just looked at me with a determined look in his eyes. Then I broke his stare to glance around. Maybe I was expecting the people around me to point out the hidden candid cameras to me and reveal this whole thing as a cheap gag. But no one was paying any attention to me at all.

"Will you do it? Will you pretend for me?"

"A million dollars?" I repeated, trying to wrap my head around the enormity of what he was offering me. It felt as if I had fallen into a rabbit hole. These kinds of things just did not happen to me.

"Yes, and you get everything that comes with living my life-style," he explained. "Money, free time, travel… anything you want. You just have to stand there and look pretty on my arm when I go to events, that's it."

"That sounds a little too good to be true," I said, not letting myself get carried away.

"A million dollars and a few months of your life," he urged. "You just have to make sure that you keep this a secret forever, and you get the money."

"What about Lorraine? I must tell her."

He frowned. "No."

I was clear. "I won't do it if I can't tell her."

He sighed. "Okay. You can tell her, but you must get her to promise not to tell anyone else."

I paused, taking in what he'd just said to me. I would get to come to events like this all the time, whenever I felt like it. This world would be open to me. I wouldn't be an outsider anymore. I would be on the arm of this gorgeous, rich, successful man. And for only a few months work I'd get a million dollars. Wow! This would change everything for me. And for Lorraine. We could afford a new apartment. I could to go to college, and get my degree, to pursue the career I was really passionate about.

"I'll do it," I blurted out, not even sure what I was saying. I didn't know if I actually truly believed him, or if I thought this was all a load of crap that would later come out as a bald-faced lie, but look what was at stake? No more having to put up with snooty customers, no more worrying about creepy Joe screaming at me over the serving counter, or having my pay docked for breaking their expensive china. But the best part was I would get to play at being the wife of this gorgeous, successful man. Yeah, I could live with that.

"Excellent," he replied smoothly, his eyes shining as though he had just pinned down the deal of a lifetime. He took his phone out. "Give me your number and my secretary will be in touch tomorrow to take you shopping."

My eyes widened. This just got better and better. "Shopping?"

"I think a new wardrobe might be in order," he explained. "Not that you don't look great, but if you're going to fit in with my crowd..."

"Yeah, yeah, I get it," I agreed, thinking back to the sweats and tee I was wearing before I'd come out.

"We can meet for dinner to go over the details," he continued. "If that works for you?"

"That works great for me," I replied. I couldn't believe I was doing this. Was it really happening? I didn't even know that I believed it, not entirely, but he kept smiling at me, his face warm and inviting, and I suddenly felt the urge to lean forward and kiss him. Which was crazy, because I barely knew him, but at the same time not at all, because I would be marrying him soon. If this scheme he was selling was anywhere close to the truth.

"Here you go." He handed me his phone.

I tapped in my number quickly before I handed it back to him.

I realized I was just standing there in the middle of the floor. Suddenly, I could feel Lorraine's eyes burning into the back of my head. "Right. I guess I better get back to Lorraine."

"Want me to escort you back?"

I shook my head slowly.

"See you at dinner tomorrow?"

"See you at dinner tomorrow," I echoed. I think I was still in a daze.

He nodded formally then turned and disappeared into the crowd.

CHAPTER 7

Slowly, I turned back to see Lorraine gesturing excitedly for me to come over to her.

For second, I didn't move at all. The rest of the room fell away and all I could see was Lorraine. Dear Lorraine. She was the one who brought me here so she deserved at least some of the cash I was going to get from this deal... if it was real, which I wasn't sure of yet. As I watched, I saw her face change, her expression looking worried. I grinned suddenly and all the joy of earlier came back instantly.

"Hey, hey, hey!" she exclaimed happily when I made my way back over to join her. "Did I see you giving Gabe Grayson your number?"

"Who is he?" I whispered.

"What? You don't know who he is? If I wasn't living with you, I would think you've been living in a cave in North Korea."

"Who is he?" I asked again.

"Unbelievable." She shook her head. "He has been voted the most eligible billionaire by GQ three years running and you've never heard of him! Anyway, please tell me you are seeing him again?"

I opened and closed my mouth, trying to find shape to the words that just wouldn't come out. I smiled at her, finally, and took a deep breath, readying myself for what came next. This would change everything. I couldn't wait to share it with her. "Lorraine," I announced. "I think there's something I need to tell you."

I moved forward, and cupping my hand over her ear, hit her with the incredible news. When I pulled back, her mouth was open.

"Oh, sweet baby Jesus! This is big! This is real big. Are you sure he was serious?"

"I think he was," I replied. "But I guess we'll find out tomorrow when his secretary calls. Or doesn't."

"A million dollars," she breathed, like she was afraid it would get frightened and fly away if she made too much noise around it. "That's an insane amount of money. Think of everything you could do with that..."

"That *we* could do," I corrected.

She cocked her head at me. "What are you saying, Willow?"

"I want to give you half," I explained.

Her eyes looked like they were going to roll right out of her head. "You're kidding," she gasped. "You can't give me—that much. T-that's too much. It wouldn't be fair. I mean—"

"I want you to have it, Lor," I stated firmly. "If this turns out to be true. I wouldn't be here at all if it wasn't for you, remember? I have you to thank for all of this. You're the one who got that invitation and blackmailed me into going."

"That's true, but still."

"No buts. We're like sisters. That's what sisters do for each other."

"No they don't. I know of sisters who kill each other for less money."

"Can you stop it? We're sharing the money and that's it. That's if he was not messing with my head."

"But—"

"Just think what you can do with the money, Lor. Haven't you always wanted to start your own boutique?"

"True, but you're my best friend, and if you think I'm just going to let some random guy slide in and steal you away from me, then you've got another thing coming," she told me with no room in her voice for argument.

"I ain't going nowhere, babe. More than ever, I'll need someone who can keep me sane."

"Do I get to be your Maid of Honor?" she asked, leaning over and clasping my hands excitedly.

I grinned. "Of course."

"This calls for a drink," she shouted happily, and waved down a bartender. He was there in a split-second. She ordered margaritas and told him to make them double strong.

"To fake marriages," I announced, lifting my glass to clink it against hers.

"To fake marriages," she echoed, a mad giggle escaping her throat.

I started laughing too.

The rest of the night passed in a blur, with the two of us drinking and dancing with each other. Now that I understood there wasn't a person here who didn't know we were gatecrashers, I didn't care anymore about pretending to be someone else. Lorraine declared it my unofficial bachelorette party. Such a hilarious concept to me, but I went along with it, letting loose in a way I hadn't in ages. We ended up having an awesome time. The last thing I remember was Lorraine dancing on the bar counter.

****

I woke up the next morning, more than a little worse for wear with my feet throbbing like mad. The night before seemed like a dream. An impossible dream. Part of me still believed it could be true, but rational side of me knew it must have been a joke. It had to be some kind of joke, some sick, twisted game that he played to get women into bed with him. Though it was a hell of an elaborate story to concoct if there really was no use for it...

Since he never even tried to get me in bed.

I reached over and grabbed my phone, blearily peering at the screen so I could check the time. I didn't have work today, at least, so I didn't have to worry about rolling onto a bus to make it to my shift on time. Instead, I found myself staring at a message.

A message from the secretary of none other than Gabe Grayson.

CHAPTER 8

GABE

I sat in the restaurant unsure if she would even turn up.

This had to be one of the most spectacularly harebrained things I'd ever done. I didn't know her from Eve. She could easily go to the press or to someone who worked with me, bust open my whole scheme, exposing me completely, and ruin my reputation. And yet, here I was, sitting in one of the most exclusive restaurants in Chicago, waiting for a woman I barely knew who I was planning to make my wife as soon as possible.

What could go wrong?

Tina, my secretary, had set up the appointment for me, and sent her on a shopping trip with a personal shopper. Not like there was any hurry to get her a wardrobe today, but it was a softening tactic. What woman doesn't like to shop? Besides, I wanted to keep her busy and not thinking until I could talk to her tonight.

She could still bail on me, take the clothes and run, or she could come along to tell me she can't do it, but the one thing I'd learned very early on was... money talks. The deal I was offering was too sweet for most girls to say no to.

I put my drink on the bar counter and saw her being led in by the hostess.

Jesus, she looked good enough to eat. Wearing a blue dress and heels, her hair was loose and wild down her back, totally different from all the uptight hairstyles that populated the place. I stood as she approached.

She slipped into the seat next to me with ease. "Hey," she greeted, a little shyly, as though she wasn't quite sure what she was meant to say. Then she smiled. Her smile was slightly crooked, but that just gave her face a little more character. In the upper echelons of this city, I was so used to seeing people groomed to perfection that I'd almost forgotten what it was like to be around someone who was just normal. It was almost a relief, knowing that she was as real as they came. Even if I was asking her to be my fake wife.

"Hey," I replied. "Good to see you again, Willow."

"I didn't know you were *the* Gabe Grayson."

"Yeah," I said mockingly. "That's me, *the* Gabe Grayson."

"Gabe Grayson," she repeated, as though she was testing out how the word felt on her tongue. "Well, it's nice to finally meet you properly, future husband."

The words caught me off-guard, even though I had engineered it all. The idea of marriage was still a foreign, unfamiliar concept. I hadn't even given it a thought until last night.

45

She raised her eyebrows at me when she noted my reaction. "Is that still on? Did I hallucinate that entire thing?"

I shook my head. "No, you sure didn't. I'm glad you brought it up. There's a lot that we need to go over before we get this started. Let me get you a drink first. What's your poison?"

"A glass of white wine would be nice."

I ordered the drink and turned back to her.

"Yeah, I've never done the whole arranged marriage thing before, so I think you're going to have to let me know what the etiquette is," she remarked.

I glanced around with a frown. In my position, even the walls had ears. "Keep your voice down," I whispered. "The most important part of our bargain is that you maintain complete secrecy. I cannot stress enough how important that is. You or your friend can never talk about this to anyone or the deal is off and you don't get a penny."

"Sorry, sorry," she apologized. "I wasn't thinking. It's just... this is a lot to take in. Especially with your... background."

It occurred to me again: she really did have the most beautiful eyes. They seemed to light up her whole face, making it radiant. "So, you've been doing some research?"

Her drink arrived and she took a sip. "Yeah, well, I like to at least know something about the guy I'm going to jump into a wedding with," she replied with a grin. "Your resume is pretty impressive though."

"Sure is," I replied.

She laughed. "Not afraid of coming across as cocky, huh?"

I shrugged. "Don't see any reason to play down my achievements since I worked my ass off to get them."

She glanced at me sideways and fire raced through my system. I hadn't noticed it before, but she had the most beautiful grey eyes. Pale and bright, all at the same time. The soft makeup she wore accentuated her full lips, natural and not overly plumped with fillers or injections.

I caught myself in my line of thought. *No, no, don't go there Gabe. If this is going to work, you can't complicate it with sex.* I cleared my throat. "Right, let's get down to the specifics of this deal."

"That's how every woman dreams of being proposed to," she shot back, clasping her hand to her heart as though it was more than she could take. She had a sense of humor, which didn't please me in the least. I didn't want to be attracted to her. To make this work, I had to set the rules down clearly. We are not lovers. We are not friends. We are business associates.

A waiter approached with menus for us. I told him we were ready to go to our table and he immediately led us into the restaurant proper.

I noticed a few people watching us covertly from their tables, probably wondering what the hell I was doing here. I had a bit of a reputation around this city—all right, a *big* reputation —and it wasn't for sweeping girls out for romantic dinner dates every chance I got. In fact, word was starting to get around I might not be straight, or have some other perversion that couldn't be made public.

Willow ordered a creamy pasta dish, which was another first

for me. I couldn't remember the last time I had been out on a date and the woman had ordered anything but the lowest-calorie salad with a pained expression on her face.

When the wine was poured into our glasses and the waiter slinked off, I leaned in to tell her about the deal I had in mind. I told her the relationship would only last for as long as it had to, the time span I was thinking of was a maximum of a year. I was sure of that. Certainly, I wasn't committing to anything beyond what I utterly had to. For as long as it took the lawyers to make it all nice and legal. I'd already done some research on surrogates and had a few clinics that I was sure would match my needs well. My most discreet lawyer was already at work on the contracts we would need to pull this whole thing off. Everything would be above-board, strictly business, completely platonic. There would be nothing, absolutely nothing going on between us beyond what we had to do in public to convince everyone that we were madly in love.

"Right," she said, once I had finished my long spiel. "What happens after we're actually married? Where will I live?"

"You'll move in with me, of course," I replied immediately. "I have plenty of spare rooms at my place, and we'll get one of them set up for you."

"And I'm assuming this also means that I'll be giving up my job?"

"Of course," I replied. "Naturally, I'll cover all living expenses that come up while you're staying with me and you'll have a monthly allowance for shopping and stuff. This would be on top of the agreed final settlement."

"Well, then…" She leaned back in her seat while staring at me as though she couldn't quite believe that this was happening, "I don't think I have any other questions."

"So it's safe to say that you're on board from here on out?" I asked eagerly.

She hesitated, but only for a moment, and then nodded. "Yes, I think it's safe to say I am."

I almost wanted to rub my hands together with the sensation of victory I felt. *There you go, granddad. Problem solved and thanks for nothing.* I smiled at her. "Great. We can figure out what we're going to do about the actual wedding part of it before then, but for now, I think we've come as far as we can. I'll make sure you have the contracts by early next week, maybe even before…"

"You're going to at least let me finish my meal first, right?" she asked playfully, pointing at the delicious plate of food that had recently arrived in front of her.

"I'm sure I could see it in my heart to," I teased.

She giggled and her cheeks became suddenly rosy. Her gaze slid away from me, as if looking me in the eyes was proving a little too difficult. She dropped her voice to a whisper. "I think that's the least you could do, seeing I'm going to be wearing a belly bump for a few months," she pointed out before tucking into her food happily. She closed her eyes and chewed. "Oh, my God," she gushed. "You have no idea how freaking delicious this is."

I smiled at how natural and unguarded her reaction was. It was almost like watching a child.

As we chatted over our food, I was surprised to note that I was actually enjoying her company. She was smart, well-spoken, and had this goofy sense of humor unlike anything I encountered in the carefully-cultivated corporate world I exclusively moved in. It was actually a wonderful thing to be around someone who was clearly without any hidden agenda, as opposed to someone who was secretly trying to wring me for everything I had. Her brand of vulnerability and openness seemed so magnetic that I had to remind myself again and again, that this was still a business relationship, and I would do well to remember this in the coming months.

All too soon, the meal ended. I'd even treated myself to dessert. I told myself I was putting on a good show for anyone paying attention to my date. I had to sell the whirlwind romance shit relatively convincingly if I intended to get through this without arousing any major suspicion, but the truth was I had dessert because she'd said with a hopeful look on her face, *"I'll only have one if you do too."*

When we were ready to go, I got to my feet and went to help pull her chair out, but my hand dropped too quickly and my fingers brushed over her bare arm. Her skin felt so silky under my fingers that for a fraction of a second, I forgot this was meant to be nothing more than a business deal.

Willow caught her breath and stiffened.

I swiftly pulled my hand away from her and stepped back. "I'll speak to you again soon," I quickly interjected, before the tense silence grew too intense.

She nodded and got to her feet, glancing away from me. "Yes, right, of course."

I made a small gesture with my palm. "Shall we?"

She headed towards the entrance.

Outside, in the cool night air I turned to her. "Do you need a lift home? My driver could drop you off."

"No. I'll just get a taxi. Thank you for dinner."

"Look, let my driver drop you off. I've got a conference call in a couple of hours, so I'm just going to go back to the office. It's a five-minute walk."

She hesitated.

"It would make me feel better knowing you will be safely taken home."

She sank her teeth into that plump bottom lip. "All right."

I led her to my car.

Brad, my driver, jumped out of the car and held the door open for her.

I didn't try to touch her. I just stood back stiffly and said goodnight.

The car pulled away, leaving me standing there in the cool night air, with nothing but the feeling of her warm, soft skin against mine for company. I shook my head with disgust with myself. What the hell was I doing?

So, she's a looker. So what?

There were plenty of beautiful women in this city I could hook up with if I wanted to. No matter what kind of attraction I felt for her, nothing was going to happen. I could never jeopardize my plan because I couldn't keep my dick in my pants. Grayson Inc. was far too important to me. It was what I had worked for all my life.

I already knew I was flying pretty close to the sun as it was… coming up with this crazy scheme.

CHAPTER 9

WILLOW

I swallowed and glanced at the registrar. He kept looking at me expectantly.

I wiped my hand down the white sheath dress I was wearing. I wriggled my toes. My feet were killing me, and that was Lorraine's fault. She insisted I buy these baby blue heels that perfectly matched the little soft blue roses in my hair. As my Maid of Honor, she insisted that looks were more important than comfort.

I glanced at her. Clutching a bouquet of peonies, she kept watching me with a huge smile on her face. I could practically see the dollar signs pulsing in her eyes, and I reminded myself that this was why I was getting married. To make a better life for myself and for my best friend.

That had been all that mattered from the moment Gabe came up with his crazy proposition at that fancy party. Then it was a non-stop whirlwind of activity. Gabe had said I would get the papers in a week; as it turned out I was at his attorney's office within two days. It was a long contract, thirty pages long. They left the room so I could read it. I started reading and gave up at the second page. It was so full of jargon. I went back out and asked the attorney if he thought he had drawn up a fair agreement.

He said he had followed Gabe's instructions to the letter.

That was good enough for me. I signed the papers and made our agreement a formal contract. After that, it got crazy. His super-efficient personal assistant set up a day for me to go out shopping to gather everything I might need for the life-style that was ahead of me, the clothes, the accessories, the makeup, the perfume, everything.

I searched on the net to see if there was anything in the way of etiquette lessons in the city, but I didn't find anything so I decided to just hope I didn't do anything too spectacularly stupid.

The hasty, simple wedding turned out to be more complicated than I could have possibly imagined. It included some fancy PR footwork of getting some "leaked" photos and stories planted in some celebrity magazines so that the press would pick up on the story and run with it.

Which they seemed to do a lot when it came to him.

After a while, it felt as if my life was no longer my own. I was constantly on show. I started to meet people as Gabe's wife-soon-to-be. Snooty people who thought they were better than me. Gabe promised that once we got married, everything would die down and we could settle down to a more private existence.

So here I was, standing before him in the middle of a civil ceremony pledging my life to him for a million bucks. In terms of money, it was barely a drop in the ocean to him, at least according to the estimates I'd found of his wealth online.

He wasn't exactly hurting for cash… let's put it that way.

One of his staff gave me a tour of his insanely luxurious apartment on the expensive side of Chicago, and I swear my jaw was dragging on the expensive granite floor as we went from room to room. The place was amazing; huge, airy and perfectly decorated. I tried to imagine him lounging around here eating expensive fruit from glass bowls or whatever it was rich people did with their time and I couldn't. The place looked as if it was a showroom. No one lived here.

When I told Lorraine about it, she promised to check in often to make sure that I was still safe and comfortable where I was. I assured her there was nothing wrong with his place, that if she'd seen it she would have been clawing my eyes out to get in instead of me, but she held firm.

It was odd to think that I wouldn't be living with her for almost a whole year. She'd been my roommate since we'd both moved to this city around the same time and happened to pull each other in an apartment lottery.

I smiled back at Lorraine and turned my gaze back to Gabe.

Hopefully, I was selling my part as the blushing bride, as the registrar continued to drone through the rest of the service. I said my *I do* when the time was right. He looked deep into my eyes as he said the words right back to me, and I felt a twist deep in my gut. I wasn't sure why, but something about this man committing himself to me, utterly and completely, even if it was only as part of this charade we were playing, flicked a switch inside of me.

I'd been doing my best to hold back the raw attraction I felt for him and keep myself from doing anything physical with him, but honestly, in that moment, I understood fully the meaning of the phrase 'wanting to jump someone's bones.'

"You may now kiss the bride," the registrar announced, beaming at us.

Gabe moved forward and brushed his lips over my cheek, at the very corner of my mouth, a kiss that looked chaste, but only if you weren't looking too closely. Because his lips burned my skin and when he pulled back, I could feel the spot he had touched me with his lips throbbing.

Every time he touched me, I couldn't shake the feeling that we were meant to be something more. More than just this fakery, more than just this game we were playing to outwit his grandfather.

As soon as the ceremony was over, we headed out of the registry and back to his apartment. His secretary had arranged for all the new stuff I had purchased to be transferred to his apartment, much to my relief, because I already felt the toll the day was taking on me, weighing heavily on my shoulders.

CHAPTER 10

WILLOW

"**Y**ou okay?" Gabe asked a little stiffly, from the other side of the limo.

I nodded and smoothed my white dress over my knees. I didn't know what to think, how to feel. I wished I could have been with Lorraine right now, just to talk all of this out and get my head on straight, but I was with my new husband. I had to find some way to keep myself together. "Yeah, I'm fine," I assured him. "Just... can't believe this is really happening, that's all."

"Hey, don't get too worried," he warned me with a smile. "It's not going to be for long. As soon as the contracts are signed over in my name, you're back to the real world."

"Right," I agreed, even though admitting this stung a little. I wasn't sure why I felt that way. It wasn't as if he'd promised me anything different. Yet, there was a part of me, a small, very tiny part of me, that didn't want this to be that easy for him.

"Okay, we're here," he remarked as the driver pulled the door open on my side. Before I could get out, he was already at my side, holding a helping hand out to me. A couple of people glanced at us as we headed towards the apartment, the bride and groom, fresh from our wedding. I plastered a happy smile on my face and hoped that none of them were looking too closely.

When we got into the apartment, it was deathly quiet.

Gabe turned towards me and rubbed the back of his neck with his hand. "Look, I have to get back to the office." He gestured towards the main living area. "You have everything you need in the kitchen for a quick sandwich, but if you want a proper meal or anything, just call the chef."

"You have a chef?" I gasped. I knew he was rich, but I didn't realize he was quite *that* rich.

"Yeah, he's on the extension list next to the door," he replied, shrugging, as though it should have been obvious. "I'll be back late. So go ahead and make yourself at home." He turned to head to the door, but before he did, he paused and glanced up at me, and I don't know why but my heart skipped a beat.

"Oh, and put some of your clothes in the closet in my room," he told me. "Just in case anyone comes snooping."

"Sure," I agreed.

He smiled at me, his hand on the door. "Thanks for doing this for me."

"No problem," I said, and watched as he went out and closed the door. I retreated to the space that would be mine for the foreseeable future. I pretended to be glad to have a little time to myself to think.

I went and sat on the bed that looked like it probably cost more than a full year of tips I made at the restaurant. From where I sat, I could see the walk-in wardrobe that was by now, no doubt, populated with all the fancy garments Lorraine and I had picked out. Suddenly, I felt quite sad. I never thought my wedding day would be like this. When I was reading all those romance books, I had dreamed of something special for me.

I walked over to the wardrobe, opened it, and cast my eye over the row of heels. Most of them were chosen by Lorraine. A small box of my own clothes had been tucked away at the far end of the wardrobe, and I went to grab a few bits and pieces, stripping hurriedly out of my wedding dress and tossing it aside. It crumpled on the floor like a napkin.

I pulled on my comfortable sweats and felt slightly better.

I decided to make myself a sandwich. In my bare feet, I made my way to the kitchen. I opened the fridge and it was indeed, richly stocked with all kinds of food. I made myself a cheese sandwich and took it to the vast living room. Putting my glass of orange juice and plate on the coffee table, I opened the sliding door and went out onto the balcony. It was quite cool, but it felt nice.

I ate my sandwich alone on the balcony.

I washed my plate and glass and put them away. Then I went back to the big black sofa and sat down. It was surprisingly comfortable and before I knew it, I had fallen asleep. When I woke up it was dark. For a second, I didn't know where I was and it startled me, but then I remembered.

I thought of Gabe, working at his office. What a strange man. If I had the money he had, I would never work as hard as he did. I would be out enjoying my life, not trying to earn more shekels to add to the shekels I couldn't possibly spend in my lifetime.

I stretched and made my way to the bathroom. All my new makeup and toiletries were waiting for me there. I decided to take a shower with the crazy-expensive soap I'd been persuaded to buy, the kind made with jasmine and amber, or so the woman at the counter claimed.

It was one of those luxurious ceiling mount showerheads. I stood under it and closed my eyes. The steam rushed around me and distantly, I heard someone moving in the apartment. I recognized the footfalls at once. It had to be him, back at last. I wondered if I should go out and greet him, play the dutiful wife, but what would be the point? It wasn't like there was anyone around to see us, and my guess was he probably just wanted to be left alone.

But still.

The two of us were alone together, in this apartment, husband and wife, on our wedding night, no less. Not that I intended to let my brain stray to any untoward places, but if I did, now was the time. I washed myself carefully, letting the silky bubbles run down my skin as I listened intently to him outside.

Slowly, I found my hand trailing down between my legs. I knew this was dangerous, that I was indulging in an attraction to him that I should never have allowed myself to have in the first place, but I didn't care. I skimmed my fingers over my clit and let out a moan, cloaked by the sound of the water tumbling down around me.

What if I just went out there and asked him to join me? How

would he react? Maybe he would just laugh in my face and tell me to get my shit together, that our marriage was nothing other than a business arrangement.

Or maybe...

I let my mind stray. In my head, he climbed into the shower beside me. Sliding his hands around my body, he brushed my fingers away from between my legs and replaced them with his own. He pulled my hips back so the jet of water was directly against my pussy, as he stroked me, held me and kissed up and down along my shoulder and my neck, his slick, strong body tense against mine...

I could hear him moving around outside, and it was almost enough for me to convince myself that he was headed in my direction. I didn't know what he'd been doing while he was out of the house. Probably working his ass off, but in my mind, I convinced myself that he had spent the time thinking about me, about touching me, holding me, having me. I remembered his lips against my cheek at the ceremony, and I could have sworn I felt that spot burning once again. I grabbed the free-standing shower head and pulled it down to my pussy, allowing the pulsing pummel of the jets to tip me over the edge. I clamped my hand over my mouth to muffle the cry that erupted from my mouth as my orgasm ricocheted through me.

I caught my breath and returned the shower head to its spot, hoping that he hadn't heard me, or that if he had... some part of me wanted him to take it as the open invitation it was. But the sane part of me, the stronger part, the part in control, knew better than to let myself indulge my feelings for him.

That would be batshit crazy.

A man like him was out of bounds to me. The only time he would go for someone like me was if it was part of some bizarre, twisted-up game like the one he was playing with his late grandfather's estate right now.

Things were already complex enough, and the last thing I needed was to add another complication in the form of sex onto this highly unusual situation.

CHAPTER 11

GABE

I woke early the next morning, before the sun had even risen, and stared out at the softly-lit city beyond my window. It was pretty in this light with the pinks and deep hues of the almost-dawn.

A dream lingered in the back of my mind. I closed my eyes. I couldn't quite remember it, but there were flickering memories dancing over my mind. Grey eyes, soft, full lips curled up into a smile. The feeling of hands on my body, silky skin against my hardness, soft hair brushing over my chest.

I pushed the images to the back of my mind. I knew precisely who it was about and the last thing I needed was to indulge in the dumb little fantasies I'd been allowing my overheated brain to make about my wife. My eyes snapped open. She was not *my* wife as such. She was just my pretend wife.

And there was a damn good reason for it.

We hadn't even spent our wedding night together, for God's sake. I did consider offering her a drink when I arrived home last night to celebrate our union, or more appropriately, the deal, but I heard the shower running and I didn't want to disturb her. Besides, the thought of the warm water coursing all over her curves was more than I could take, distinctly dangerous to my current state of mind.

I stretched and rolled out of bed. Grabbing some clothes, I pulled them on as I headed to the kitchen. My plan was to get a glass of water, then head down to the gym to squeeze in a workout for an hour, hopefully burn off some of the excess energy that was clearly giving me strange and unwelcome ideas about Willow.

I was greeted by a sight that caused a different kind of thirst. A raging thirst.

Willow was standing by the island with her back to me, her long hair loose and wild over her shoulders and wearing nothing but a strappy top and a matching pair of pale pink panties. They looked gorgeous against her perfectly pale skin and her butt looked incredible; even if I didn't want to admit it to myself, the way her curvy body filled out her skimpy attire was making me want to reach out and sink my fingers into that peachy ass...

"Oh!" she squeaked, whirling around to face me.

Apparently, she'd been eating a bowl of cereal, holding it in her hand as she munched and stared out of the tall windows. Then she jerked with shock when I startled her, as the milk jumped out of her bowl and splashed down the front of her thin silk top.

In a split-second, I could make out the outline of her breasts and her hardened nipples.

Fuck! I couldn't stop staring.

"I'm sorry, I didn't mean to wake you," she blurted out, grabbing a towel and mopping at herself.

I wanted to pull my gaze away. I swear I wanted to, but I stood there like a man mesmerized. I could see her breasts perfectly through the transparent top. I wanted to throw her up against a wall and lick her clean myself. The thought was so lewd, the image so intensely vivid, that it even took me by surprise.

I tore my gaze away from her, forcing my attention onto something, anything. I stared stupidly at the polished granite top of the island counter.

"I'm really sorry," she said again.

"You didn't..." I muttered. I realized that my averted face would be as much of a giveaway to my attraction as actually looking at her would. "I was just... uh, I was just getting myself something to drink. I'm headed to the gym. Doesn't matter. I'll get some there."

"No, don't do that. I'll get out of your hair," she said quickly, and immediately shot past me in the direction of her bedroom.

Even though I knew I shouldn't, I turned to watch her go. I was almost overwhelmed by the urge to ask her to stay.

No, more than that. I wanted to reach out and grab her lush body, touch her, fuck her, lift her up on to the island top, open her legs, and screw her till she screamed my name. I wanted to peel the sopping fabric off her skin and expose her. I wanted to see all of her, use her, and make her mine, more than I did the day before when I'd married her.

What was a marriage without consummation, right...?

But I stopped myself before I made a fool of myself. What the fuck is going on in my head? This wasn't what I had signed up for. Quite the opposite, actually. I was meant to barely see her beyond what we needed to do to convince other people we were the real deal. Yet, here I was, feeling as though I might lose control in my own house. All because she was a little scantily-clad?

If she hadn't walked out, I would have had to, just to keep my shit together. That was how into her I was.

That was how badly I wanted her.

Which was insane. Because she wasn't my type. She wasn't anything like the women I normally went for; she didn't come from the same lifestyle, didn't move in the same circles, didn't bother with the same kind of people. We were a terrible match for one another, apart from the fact I wanted to fuck her brains out.

I needed to get a grip. This was only day two. If I carried on this way, it would all go to hell in a hand-basket. It would only work as long as we both stuck to our side of the agreement and that didn't involve, for one second, acting on a fleeting attraction.

Willow was just a girl, after all. Just a girl. I could find one of them whenever I wanted to. What mattered was that she was the key to getting the business I knew I deserved. The business I had worked all my life to get. That was my ultimate goal. Not her.

CHAPTER 12

WILLOW

As I hurried back to my room, I couldn't help but see the look on his face. It was as though he had been actually, truly furious at me for being there. I wasn't sure whether I was more embarrassed, or hurt, or just completely infuriated about the whole thing.

He said to make myself at home. I hadn't intended to wake him when I'd gone through for something to eat, but I had woken early in this unfamiliar place and I knew that breakfast would make me feel a little more at home here. How was I to know he would wake up at dawn and come to the kitchen? Anyway, I would have been wearing less if I'd been in a bikini on a beach.

What had I done that was so wrong?

After all, he was the one who'd come up with this entire proposition. He was the one who had wanted me to marry him, come here, live with him and play at being his wife. And he had been perfectly–well, maybe sweet was an overstatement, but he had been perfectly pleasant and polite until this morning.

I frowned. Earning the million dollars looked like it might be a whole lot harder than I had imagined. I didn't want to believe that. All this effort for nothing. So I tried to find excuses for him.

Maybe it was just that I had caught him first thing in the morning; he said he was heading off to the gym, but maybe he wanted to be alone. Maybe he wasn't much used to having women hanging out at his place. When I was looking around the apartment, I never saw a single sign that any woman had ever left her mark in his life. In fact, I got the feeling that I might have been one of the only women he'd actually brought back to this place and certainly one of the rare ones who'd been allowed to stay more than one night.

I sat at the edge of my bed, staring sullenly out through the window. Eventually, I went to the window and looked to the street below. People were just starting to go out and head off to work— suddenly, I found myself missing Lorraine and our cozy little flat. I had even quit my job. What on earth was I going to do all day here on my own? What reason would there be to get out of bed every morning?

At that moment of self-pity, I almost felt nostalgic for the stingy customers who didn't want to leave a tip because I was such a lousy waitress, or Leo's screaming hysterically because I got an order wrong and being able to bitch it out with Lorraine. We always had fun sharing our stories of shitty customers, trying to outdo one another with who'd had the worst day, who'd had to deal with the most absurd demand.

68

I shot her off a text, but I knew she would still be sleeping after her shift last night.

I listened to Gabe as he headed out of the apartment and down the stairs, then let out a breath. Okay, so I didn't have to worry about running into him again, at least until he got home at the end of the day. I didn't want to have to see him, not until I'd had a chance to get my head a little straighter about what the hell was going on here.

Because all of this seemed to be such a mess.

Yes, I felt attracted to him, but as soon as he had laid eyes on me this morning, he had practically made a dash for the front door, like he couldn't stand to spend even one second with me. So, it was clear the feeling was far from mutual. This was a bad start to my year with him and I wasn't sure exactly how long I would be able to take it.

Quite frankly, the way I was feeling right now, he could stick his million dollars where the sun didn't shine if he was planning to treat me the way he did this morning for the rest of our year together.

I sighed and got to my feet, wandering through to the closet which was full of the most beautiful clothes I'd ever seen in my life. And I didn't have anywhere to wear them. I wished there was somewhere I could go, something I could do, that would justify me throwing on some of these absurdly beautiful clothes.

Maybe I could put on the fitted pantsuit and go down to a coffee shop nearby? But shit, I didn't even have a set of keys yet, there would be no way to do that and get back in without him. I was stuck in the apartment, with no entertainment, no friends, no work to do. How the fuck would I pass the time?

I wandered through the house for a while, picking at the food in the fridge and peering out the window on to the streets below and reading, but I couldn't concentrate. Eventually, I snuck into his bedroom, peering around and taking it in. That's when I stuck my head into his en-suite bathroom, and gasped.

There was a Jacuzzi in there, a huge, sprawling chunk of marbled ceramic with jets studded around the inside. It looked amazing... I instantly felt the urge to climb in and douse myself in warm, comforting water. It was his bath, but he did say I could make myself at home.

I decided, *fuck it.* I intended to give this a go.

I could bathe and wash myself, then clean up afterwards, well before he got back. It was only early evening and he once told me that he was such a workaholic he never got in before 10:00 pm.

He would never even know I'd been here.

We didn't have a bath at the apartment I shared with Lorraine, as there was only a shower in my bathroom, and I would be damned if I was just going to skip out on the chance to climb into the most luxurious bathtub I'd ever seen in my life.

The upsides of pretending to be married to a billionaire, huh?

I ran the bath until the water was lapping and bubbling up the sides. Then I got naked and slowly melted under the surface of the warmth. As lovely heat enveloped me, I let out a little moan of pleasure. Water coursed all over my body. It was the most incredible sensation ever.

If I were him, I would only get out of this thing to eat, sleep and use the bathroom. It was far too comfortable, far too pleasing. I would conduct all my meetings in here, surrounded by investors and partners as the steam rose around me.

I fiddled with the controls for the jets and flicked their different settings, and the water clouded with a rush of energy, pummeling my sore muscles. My calves were aching from where I'd been in heels the whole day before. Something about being surrounded by all this luxury made me feel as though I had to indulge myself, too. I held one of my feet suspended over one of the jets.

"Oh yesssssss…."

Yeah, I could get used to this. And as long as I could keep my head on straight, I could survive living with Gabe. No matter how confusing I found him.

CHAPTER 13

J esus, what a fucking day. I felt like I had been running around half-crazy since I'd gotten out of bed and yet I hadn't really achieved anything.

Well, at least people knew about the wedding now. I had made a point of flashing my ring around as much as I could, and I had fielded a few questions on the issue, letting everyone know that yes, I was in love and yes, it had been spontaneous and yes, of course, it was real, how could you even imply that I'd do anything else? I'd reached out to the surrogacy agency again, and done my best to keep my mind off Willow and her soaked, sheer top.

Not that it had done much good.

My hands felt as though they were itching to touch her properly since I had laid eyes on her like that. It would have been so, so easy to just reach out and caress her, to pull her close to me, and feel her soft body against mine. The shape of her ass in those panties, juicy and tempting... she had those, *oh, God* curves. I had to know what they felt like. I had to know the noises she made when she came, the way her face contorted when I pleasured her...

Yeah, I hadn't got a lot done today because I'd been too busy thinking about the woman who was wearing my ring and waiting for me at home. There was something incredibly hot about this thought, thinking about her waiting for me in my home. My secretary had arranged to have another set of keys cut for her, but I had them in my pocket now, so I knew she would be hanging out in the apartment. The thought of her, in that soft top, chest wet with milk and nipples swollen to hardness. I could almost feel them in the palm of my hand, pressing up against my skin.

By the time I got home, I had to admit I was looking forward to seeing her. I wanted to... I didn't know what exactly, but I wanted to spend a little time with her. It made sense to get to know her. To make sure our chemistry actually sold to the people it mattered most to. Like Austin to start with.

Besides, I had enjoyed the time I spent with her.

I pushed open the door with an odd sort of lightness inside me. It was strange, knowing that there was someone else in this place. I walked in and her bedroom door was wide open. I walked up to it and found the room empty, the door to the bathroom was open to show that she wasn't there either. I furrowed my brow. Maybe she'd gone to see Lorraine and would call me later to pick her up.

I glanced at her bed. It was neatly made. Shaking my head at how base I had become, I left her bedroom and went into mine. Pulling off my jacket and my shirt, I tossed them on to the bed, and headed through to the bathroom.

I froze.

73

There you are, little Willow.

I walked up to the bath. She was fast asleep. And completely naked. And even though I knew I shouldn't have been staring, it was impossible for me to tear my gaze away. She just looked so damn good, all laid out like that, the soft curve of her body impossibly sexy beneath the bubbling water. The urge to touch her was so great I took a step back.

"Willow," I called my voice husky with need. My cock stirring in my pants.

Her beautiful eyes popped open. "Oh!" she squeaked. Her hair was damp and slicked down to her head, showing off her gorgeous grey eyes, her lips swollen and full.

I wanted to lean down and sink my teeth into them. And that was when I realized I was also shirtless, and that she hadn't exactly made any move to get out of the bath.

Her arms were wrapped around herself, carefully, so she was hidden from me, but she wasn't going anywhere. "I'm sorry, I didn't mean to invade your space," she blurted out. "I just—I saw you had a bath and I didn't—and I wasn't sure if I was going to..."

"It's fine," I murmured. This was dangerous, distinctly dangerous and yet, I didn't want to walk away from it. Not yet, not until I knew where this might be going. Where this ended up. "You need a hand getting out of there?" I asked my voice low.

Her eyes widened as she slowly unwrapped her arms from around her body, not taking her eyes off me once. "Yeah, I'm sure I could."

I could see the pink tips of her breasts from under the water.

Without thinking a moment longer, I leaned down and pulled her out of the bath, scooping her up into my arms and holding her against my body. I didn't care that she was dripping wet. In fact, it just made it all the easier to feel every contour of her sweet, delicious body. I wanted to run my hands all over her, touch her, feel her, fill her up.

She hooked her arms around my neck and gazed up at me, lips slightly parted.

I laid her down on the bed and laying her out on the sheets, I looked down at her wet, naked body.

She moaned and reached for me, sliding her hand behind my head and pulling me down towards her.

But instead of planting a kiss on her lips, I ducked down to her neck, brushing my lips almost tenderly along her soft, damp skin. She tasted lightly of something floral, something I wanted to feast on all day. This was crazy and I damn well knew it, but I didn't care. All I cared about was indulging in the sweetness of this moment, of getting this out of our systems before it became too intense to fight any longer.

I moved my mouth down while running my hands over her nude body. She felt so good, so delicate, so full; luxurious, almost. I adored every second of it. She moaned again and reached down to caress my hair, running her fingers over my scalp gently as I moved further and further down… to a part of her I knew I needed to taste if I intended to get her out of my head…

Finally, I arrived between her legs. I spread them wide apart and exposed the fruit between them. I let out a soft groan when I saw her pussy, glistening and pink, waiting there for me like a gift I'd never known I needed. I slipped my hands beneath her ass and pressed my mouth against her, tasting her at last.

Oh, Fuck... the taste of her drove me wild.

From the very first moment I laid eyes on her when we'd met at the party, I had known, somewhere in the back of my mind, that we would end up like this. A moment when I wouldn't be able to resist her a moment longer. When her skin would be too tempting, the perfume of her presence would grow to be too much. As I slid my tongue back and forth over her clit, caressing it slowly, I listened to her moans of pleasure.

Everything had led to this moment.

Her hands became claws in my hair as I sealed my lips around her clit and began to work the swollen bundle of nerves, softly, slowly, applying a light pressure and listening to the responses that her body gave me. I read into every muscle she tensed, every tiny noise she made, every gasp escaping her lips. I placed a hand on her belly so I could feel the rise and fall of her chest... let myself move along with it.

I stroked her with my tongue on the inhale, letting out a soft breath over her entire pussy on the exhale. I did it until her pussy began to throb and pulse. I could feel her burning for me, her pussy getting wetter and wetter as I gave all my attention to it. Desperation to get closer still clawed at my insides, my tongue sank as deep as it could into her little hole. And fuck— did her pussy feel tight. Her hips began to undulate and I felt the blood pulsing and rushing frantically in her veins.

God, she was perfect. Absolutely perfect.

I loved, no—I needed her flavor. I couldn't get enough. How had I waited so long before I'd given her, given myself, what we'd both been craving?

She clasped my head tightly and held it in place as she pushed her hips back against my mouth, greedily, as though she could hardly wait for her climax. Even as she did, I felt her body start to spasm as she rode her orgasm.

Her body arched and her muscles tensed so hard it was like they were going to snap. Her eyes rolled back and her soft moans turned into wild cries that filled the air around us. I watched it all.

She grabbed my hands and pulled me back on top of her, her eyes glazed with lust. She ran her fingers over her own nipples making them even stiffer. "I know what your tongue feels like inside me, now I want to feel your cock fill me up."

She kissed my bare chest while sliding her hands down between my legs and gripping my rock-hard cock.

"Don't move," I ordered hoarsely, and dove to my bedside table to pull a condom out of the drawer. Pulling off my pants, I kicked them aside and sheathed myself. I couldn't wait another second to plunge inside her sweet body for the first time. Getting on the bed, I quickly positioned myself over her body, her pussy open and ready to take me.

And that was when the damn doorbell rang.

CHAPTER 14

"Shit," Gabe muttered and rolled off me. He glanced at the video screen next to the bed, attached to the inter-com, and shook his head almost in disbelief when he saw who it was.

"Not ideal?" I asked.

He planted a kiss on my shoulder and went to do up his pants again. "You can say that again. It's my cousin, Austin" he replied.

"The one who gets the company if you don't produce the heir?"

"Yeah, that one. Don't worry, I'll get rid of him. It won't take long." He shot out of the bedroom.

I flopped back on the bed for a moment to catch my breath. My heart was pounding, my mind was racing, and I felt like I would explode just lying there.

In what *world* was it that he'd gotten that good at giving head? Almost as soon as he'd lowered his mouth down on me, I was ready to come. I was so satisfied but so ready for more at the same time. So ready to feel him inside me. It felt as though I had been waiting forever for him.

When he'd seen me this morning, had he wanted me then? Was that why he had left in such a hurry? Because he was worried, that he wouldn't be able to resist me? The thought of this sent another shockwave of desire through my body, the very notion of being wanted that badly by this man who himself was impossible to resist.

I listened as he invited his cousin up and buzzed him in.

"What's up," Gabe greeted curtly when he opened the door.

I got to my feet and pressing my ear to the door, I shamelessly listened to the two of them.

"What's up?" his cousin repeated. "You tell me. I heard about your shotgun wedding. Thought I would stop by and come meet the new member of the family, given that *nobody* has actually met her yet..."

Something in his cousin's voice grated on my nerves. A kind of taunting contempt. I'd met men like him before. They came into the restaurant and treated the waitresses as if were less than the dirt on their handmade shoes.

"The family will meet her... in time. For now, I'm keeping her all to myself."

"So where is she then, this mysterious woman who has swept the great Gabe off the marriage market?" he asked sarcastically.

Okay, this was my cue to come out of hiding. It was time that smug asshole got taken down a peg or two. I looked down at

Gabe's shirt lying on the floor. Yes, I could toss that on and it would look like we'd been caught in the act? And it wouldn't even be a lie. We *had* been in *the* act! It was perfect.

I pulled the shirt on as quickly as I could and strolled nonchalantly out of the bedroom. I was trying to look like the epitome of confidence even though I felt anything but. I'd hoped the first time I met his family would be a little less stressful, but I would make this work. This was what he was paying me for, wasn't it?

"Hey, baby," I crooned. I slid up next to Gabe and slipped my hand into his before standing on tiptoes to kiss his cheek. I gazed up at him with what I hoped was an adoring expression in my eyes. He squeezed my hand and I turned my head in the direction of his cousin. He looked nothing like Gabe. He had the face of a spoiled rich boy.

He gave me a hard look.

My response was to lift my hand and let the ring on my finger catch his eye. The one Gabe had picked out for me and I loved it, even though I knew it was only a fake gesture as everything about us was.

"Willow, this is my cousin, Austin. Austin, meet my wife, Willow."

"First member of the family I've met," I said, extending a hand out to him. Austin swept his eyes over me, taking me in, and I smiled at him. Gabe's shirt just fit over my body, enough to keep me concealed, but I knew it hinted at far more than it gave away. It told Austin he had interrupted Gabe and me while we were having sex.

"Great to meet you," he replied.

I could hear the insincerity and suspicion in his voice, the obvious doubt. "Same here," I replied.

Before I could say anything else, Gabe turned to me and captured my lips. He had deliberately avoided kissing me on the mouth before today, but as soon as our lips met, I felt the fireworks exploding inside of me. When he pulled back, I know had a genuinely dazed smile on my face, enough to sell our relationship to any doubting family member.

"Any reason you stopped by today?" Gabe asked him carefully. "Because I'm kind of busy at the moment..."

"Yeah, I can tell," Austin muttered. "I just wanted to tell you that there's an issue with the contracts for the Tyler-Mackenzie deal. Any chance you can come down and confirm some stuff for the guys?"

"Right, fine," Gabe agreed. "I'll be down tomorrow morning, first thing."

"Fine," Austin snapped back.

A dissatisfaction echoed in his voice that made something in me panic a little. Had he figured us out?

"Catch you later." Gabe bid him farewell, his tone cool and unperturbed. "Thanks for letting me know about the contracts."

With one last look at us, Austin nodded and backed away.

CHAPTER 15

WILLOW

Gabe pushed the door shut behind him, and let out a long breath of relief. "Jesus, that's the last time I let any of them in without getting some prior warning." He sighed. "I'm sorry. I didn't mean to spring that on you."

"I'm not. Nothing is more convincing than letting him think he interrupted us having sex. Do you think he believed us?"

"I think he'd like to think our marriage is sham, but there's nothing he can do to prove the two of us aren't madly in love."

I realized that I was still holding his hand and I withdrew it quickly, awkwardly. I didn't know how to feel right now. "What just happened?" I asked quietly.

He frowned. "With my cousin?"

"No, the other thing. Between us," I replied.

He winced and shook his head. "I'm sorry. I shouldn't have. I was just... seeing you like that... I just had to have you."

"Why are you sorry? I'm not. I had a great time," I murmured. I wasn't sure where this version of me had come from, this seductress that wanted to come out and play with the big kids.

"What are you saying?" he asked, and his gaze flicked down ever-so-briefly from my eyes to my lips.

Was he thinking about the kiss we'd just shared?

I wanted to kiss him again and again, to drink deep from the taste of him until I couldn't remember anything that came before. "We're going to be living together, right?" I pointed out. "And we're going to pretend to be married and everything. So why don't we just... lean in a little?"

"Lean in?" His voice sounded soft.

He seemed to be letting me set the pace here and I appreciated it. "We're going to spend a lot of time together in this apartment we might as well have a little fun."

His eyes darkened suggestively. "You mean..."

"I mean, we go back to that bedroom and finish what we started. If you're game, I am." I paused. "Your oral was to die for."

"Really? That's only because your pussy tasted of heaven," he said hoarsely.

I moved towards him, feeling as though I was floating slightly above the ground. I wound my arms around his neck, looked him dead in the eye, and waited for him to make the next move. I was craving it. I needed him to. I wanted to feel his sweet mouth against mine once more, to feel him touch me, caress me, and bury his head between my legs like his life depended on it all over again. "Let's go to bed," I purred, feeling like a sexy vixen.

Finally, he dipped his head down and kissed me again, properly this time, letting his tongue slide into my mouth as his hands moved softly down my waist. "Can't argue with that," he growled, as he scooped me up in his arms again and carried me through to the bedroom.

I felt so dainty and helpless when he carried me like this, exactly like the heroines in my romance novels, the way I'd always dreamed my man would. I loved the possessive way he touched me. Even though he didn't say it, his body said, mine, mine, mine. It made me feel like I was his to use and his alone.

As though I belonged to him... only him.

He laid me down on the bed and climbed on top of me, then violently tore the shirt I was wearing open to expose me completely. I giggled and wriggled, loving his hungry eyes on me, loving being the sole focus of his attention, loving how much he seemed to want me. To me it was wild that this man, who could have had any woman he wanted, was giving all his attention to me, me, me.

I could tell from the intensity in his eyes that there wasn't a single thought in in his head but me.

He made short work of taking his pants off and kicked them away. I slid up the bed, so I could get a better look at him, and I had to marvel at the sight of his utterly beautiful naked body. He was so gorgeous it actually made my heart hurt. His body was perfectly sculpted, strong, lean and toned from the gym. Every inch of him... a thing of beauty. From his biceps, his shoulders, his abs, his strong legs, and that dip that led from his hip bones towards his... impressively massive cock.

The man was hung!

He was a good eight, maybe even nine inches long and thick too, the kind of erection I'd only ever seen in pornos, but I knew I was wet enough to take every last inch of him. I couldn't wait to get that throbbing cock inside me. From the moment he had woken me up in the bathroom and I saw the bulge in his pants, I'd known where this was headed and I was ready—boy was I ready to consummate our marriage.

Something wicked tickled inside me so I grabbed my ankles and spread my legs wide giving him a view of not only my swollen, wet pussy but my asshole as well. His eyes darkened and his jaw went slack with lust. While I was open and exposed like that, I knew he couldn't tear his eyes away.

"Jesus, you're so fucking beautiful," he whispered, his voice husky.

I dropped my ankles and he grabbed a new condom, but I took it from him. I knew he was desperate to get inside me, but I wanted to make him wait. I sat up, tore the packet open carefully, and after giving his impressive cock a little teasing kiss, which made it jerk and swell, I slowly rolled it down his length. The girth of his cock filled my whole hand, and he let out the most beautiful little growl, as though my ministrations were drawing out the animal inside of him.

"Do something really bad to me," I breathed, before laying back and grabbing my ankles again.

"God, Willow," he groaned, and with a rough movement, he grabbed my hips and thrust that enormous cock into me.

For the first time, my husband was taking me on our marital bed.

"Ah!" I whimpered as he plunged the thick head into me.

My muscles felt like they had turned to jelly. The sensation of being so filled was almost painful, but he saw I was stretched wide around him, my body doing everything it could to take him in that deep, so he stopped and waited for me to get used to the invasion. In seconds, the sensation of my pussy clenched so tight around his shaft translated into pure pleasure.

I slid my hand along his back. God, he was so strong. Made me feel so safe. Looking into his eyes, I lifted my feet and hooked them over his shoulder, silently letting him know that he could go as deep as he wanted. I knew he was so big and it would hurt, but I didn't care. I wanted to ramp up the intensity.

"That is one hot little pussy you have there," he rasped, raking his teeth on my neck.

The low growl to his voice let me know that he'd been waiting for this as long as I had. We needed this. He needed me and I needed more. I was mad for his strong, lean body, so different from any man I'd hooked up with before him.

He ground my clit on the trunk of his erection. "You wanted something bad?" he taunted.

My core clenched around his dick. I could already feel an orgasm, bright and beautiful looming. "Ye—"

The word was swallowed by his mouth. His tongue dipped in, hooked my tongue and pulled it back into his mouth. He sucked it hard. His chest dragging over my nipples. I could feel the dark hairs scraping. Desperate animal grunts came from our joined mouths. Whether he was making them or I was— I didn't know.

I wasn't sure how long we stayed like that, our bodies entirely wrapped up in one another, his hands grasping for me until it bruised. A few times, I felt as though I was hovering, floating a little above the ground. Otherworldly.

Then the wet sounds of his flesh slapping on mine grew louder. My thoughts became incoherent. They blurred. A voice in my head said. *He's the one. He was always the one.* The world became glorious. I felt his cock become even bigger as he rammed so hard into me I bounced around like a doll. My sex clenched around him. I was going to come. I slipped away then and began to fly to the peak of pleasure. I heard a scream. It was me. I heard a roar. He had found his release. The noise he made when he came burned itself into my brain at once. I knew I would never get tired of it. Then he called me by name.

Everything else was pretend and fake, but this was real—the only real thing in life.

He found my lips and kissed me deeply while winding his fingers around my own like he was trying to remind me that we were still here, on earth, still together. We remained entwined, as if we were one multi-limbed beast. I knew he wasn't ready to pull out of me and I wasn't ready to let go of him either. He belonged inside my body.

"So, we're doing this?" he asked.

"We're doing this," I replied firmly. "As long as it's fun, we're doing this."

"Good." He grinned. "Because I'm not sure I would have been able to leave you alone after that."

"Well, lucky for you, I don't want to be left alone," I teased.

"Yeah, and I want to see all the erotica you have been reading put to good use," he mocked with a wicked glint in his eyes.

CHAPTER 16

WILLOW

"You sure that you actually booked the table?" Lorraine joked as we waited for the host to seat us.

I was a little nervous myself. I'd never been to such a classy place without Gabe and despite my fine clothes, some part of me was convinced they were going to take one look at me and know I was a fake who didn't belong in these lofty spaces. I was more used to serving than being served. But I drew myself up to my full height and lifted my chin in what I hoped looked confident. "Of course," I replied certainly, and sure enough, a moment later, the host appeared and took us to our seats without even me identifying myself as she called me by my name.

Oh my God, she already knew who I was.

"This way please, Mrs. Grayson."

"Wow, look at this place," Lorraine whispered, glancing around as we settled into our table. "I've heard some customers at the restaurant talking about it. Never thought I would actually come here, though."

"Well, you can thank Gabe for that," I replied. "His name opens doors like magic. Seriously. I swear, people hear my surname and they—"

"You've taken his name?" she exclaimed with surprise.

I lowered my voice. "Of course. It's part of the agreement. It's a temporary situation, but they don't know that," I pointed out with a grin.

"That's freaking crazy." Lorraine sighed. "If it wasn't you, I'd be green with envy. I had no idea how much else the agreement would bring with it. I thought it would just be getting married, scooping the cash—"

"Keep your voice down, Lor. It's supposed to be a secret," I said, almost in panic.

She clapped her hand to her mouth. "Oops…sorry."

"It's okay. Just remember that I signed an NDA and I could be hauled off to prison for breaking it."

"Okay, okay, my lips are sealed. On a different subject; it sounds like it's going to be very hard to walk away from this luxurious lifestyle. Are you going to be able to?"

I frowned, not wanting to talk about it. "I'll deal with it when I come to it."

"I suppose you're having too much fun to miss me, huh?"

Her voice sounded light, but I felt the hurt in it. "Hey, what kind of talk is that? Who sends you a text every morning? Of course, I miss you," I assured her.

"I'm sure," she snorted disbelievingly, but I could tell she was happy I hadn't abandoned her.

"You know it's true," I said. "I miss living with you. At least at our place I could leave pizza boxes out without worrying what the housekeeper will think in the morning."

"Housekeeper?" she exclaimed. "You have a housekeeper?"

"And a chef, but it's not as glamorous as what you think. To be honest, I don't like it when I trip over other people in my own home. I don't know how rich people do it, but I find it impossible to ignore them as if they are furniture or something," I confessed. Lorraine was the only person that I could be honest with all of this stuff to.

"Holy shit," she muttered. "I can pretend they are part of the furniture. Just send them over to me. Actually, if you can find me another one just like your husband, I'll take the million and everything else too, thanks so much."

"I don't think there are many others like Gabe," I replied, a little dreamily.

She raised her eyebrows at me. "Alright, now it sounds like you actually have feelings for this guy," she remarked. "But that's not true, is it?"

"I don't have *feelings* for him," I denied, making air quotes with my fingers.

Lorraine knew me too well to guess when I was spinning her a tale. Narrowing her eyes, she peered at me for a moment before she spoke again, "You're not sleeping with him, are you?"

I didn't reply.

She gasped, loudly enough to draw the attention of the couple at the table next to us.

"You are!" she exclaimed in disbelief. "Oh, my freaking God! I can't believe this. It isn't part of the deal, is it? He's not paying you for that too?"

"No, no, it wasn't and he's not paying me for that," I assured her quickly, glancing around to make sure no one was paying too much attention to us. "We're just doing it because we enjoy it. We're good together, that's all it is. Nothing more."

"Yeah, well, I'm not sure I believe that," she said bluntly.

I sighed. Truth was, I was starting to doubt myself too. I wanted to think I could separate sex from feelings, but I'd never had a casual sexual relationship before. It was always all or nothing with me. "I'm not sure I do, either," I admitted. "I mean, he's... really, really good in bed."

"Yeah, I already caught onto that one," she agreed playfully, raising her eyebrows at me.

I smiled at her. "But... I also like him. I really like spending time with him. He's smart, he's got a sense of humor, he's caring. Who wouldn't want a guy like that?"

"And you're already married to him," she reminded me. "With that contract in place."

"Yeah, I know," I agreed. I hated being reminded of that fact.

"I just want you to keep yourself safe, babe," she said gently, reaching over the table to squeeze my hand.

And I knew she meant it. She was my soul sister and wanted what was best for me. If I'd been in her position, I too, would have told her bluntly that she had to be crazy to fall for a guy like that.

But then, it wasn't easy.

Before I could come out with another word to defend myself, the waiter arrived with our menus and I decided the best course of action was to change the subject.

"So, what do you want to eat?" I asked cheerfully. I could tell she wasn't buying my overly-cheery outlook all of a sudden, but I had no intention of going back over that old ground again. It kind of hurt inside to think about the time when our contract would end and we'd have to go our separate ways.

We ate and chatted about our mutual friends, the people at the restaurant, and the drama down there, sharing gossip here and there. But every time she tried to steer the conversation back around to Gabe, or my marriage, I switched out of the subject again. I didn't want to talk to anyone about it, not even my beloved Lorraine. I was having too much fun and I wanted to live in my little fantasyland a little longer. Before it was ripped away from me.

As the meal came to a close, my phone buzzed in my purse. "Oh, give me a second," I said, grabbing it and checking who was calling me. It was Gabe. My heart skipped a beat and I took the call. "Hello?"

"Hey, are you almost finished with your meal?"

"Yeah, I guess so," I agreed. "Why do you ask?"

"I need you. Can you come to my office now? Just tell the reception desk you're my wife and one of the girls will escort you upstairs. Come straight to my office, okay?"

"Okay," I replied with a smile.

"Oh, and take your panties off before you get here."

My body began to ache to be filled by him. "Umm… see you soon."

"Was that the man of the hour?" Lorraine asked as soon as I was off the phone.

I nodded. "Yeah, it was and he wants to see me at his office. You want to get coffee, or…?"

"No, you go and see your man," she replied. "But just…" She stared at me for a moment, her brow furrowed. "Just be careful, all right? Be careful with him. And with yourself. I don't want you getting hurt. It sounds like you're falling for him."

"I will take care of myself, I promise." I smiled at her.

She frowned at me.

I reached over and squeezed her hand. "Thank you for looking out for me, but I promise you have nothing to worry about. I'll be fine."

I could tell she didn't believe me, but there wasn't much I could do about it for now. I had a meeting to make and I had a feeling we weren't going to be talking much business while I was at his office.

CHAPTER 17

GABE

I paced up and down, waiting for her to arrive. Any minute now, any minute. I didn't want to disturb her lunch, but some part of me felt jealous that she was going back to her old life. And it made me needy. It made me want to assert my claim on her too.

All morning I tried to shake her off my mind, but it proved to be a task I wasn't up for. Finally, I gave up and called her. I knew I wasn't going to be able to get down to anything productive before I showed her who she belonged to.

I heard a knock at my door and my stomach leapt.

I had brought her here last Sunday when there was no one around to show her the offices and quickly check something so she knew her way around. I yanked the door open and the woman who was playing at being my wife stood on the other side. Though, sometimes, I was finding it hard to tell the difference between fantasy and reality.

"Hey," she said softly.

I didn't bother to reply. I was just about at the end of my patience. I grabbed her hand, jerked her in, and kicked the door shut behind me. Grasping her face in one hand, I swooped down on her mouth and walked her backwards. Finally, I released her lips and kept tugging her along to my desk.

"Isn't everyone going to know what we're up to?"

"So what? You're my wife. I'll fuck you when I want to."

"Oh," Willow gasped when she hit the solidity of the desk.

I slipped my hand down between her thighs and yanked her skirt up to her waist. "I thought I told you no panties," I growled.

"I never got the chance to be alone since you called," she said with a sexy little pout.

"Disobedient little thing, aren't you?" I rasped, threading my fingers through her silky hair I tugged hard so her face was exposed to me.

"What are you going to do?" she asked.

Pure lust raged like fire inside me. "What I should have done days ago."

Her eyes widened. "What's that?"

My answer was to trace my fingers over the wet crotch of her underwear.

"Mmm..." she purred against my ear.

I watched her twist under me and felt a fierce and primal sensation of possession in my belly. No part of me could imagine another man touching her, kissing her, feeling her...

I would have loved to spend a good hour teasing and taunting her until she was begging me to fuck her, but today was not that day. I might explode before that. I dipped two fingers into her slit and felt my fingers squelch in her wetness. I drew them around to her mouth and she parted her lips at once. "Good girl," I said approving, as she tasted, sucked and lapped eagerly at my slick fingers... like obeying me was the only thing that mattered to her.

My cock sent out a rope of semen at the sight. I yanked her panties down roughly and flipped her around, pushing her over the desk so her juicy ass was arched up in the air below me. Rolling her skirt up over her hips up to her waist, I exposed all of her. I loved the way her generously curvy body looked all laid out in front of me like this.

"Fuck, you look so good like this," I said. Hell, she looks so good I wanted to bite that fleshy ass.

She wiggled her hips back and forth playfully, like she knew what she was doing to me, and I groaned. I loved it when she was like this, when she completely gave herself over to pleasure; too many women were too keen to make sure I never caught them at an unflattering angle, often twisting their bodies into unnatural positions just so they looked the way they thought looked good, not realizing it diminished our pleasure as a result. But Willow... she was different. Willow used me the way I used her, desperate and horny while focused on nothing but finding the heights of our own mutual release.

"Take me," she panted out.

I could see her trembling with need.

She looked so turned on and excited her little pussy was quivering and dripping. I unzipped my pants and sheathed myself. Inserting my index finger into her I pumped it in and out a few times to get it nice and lubricated. Then I sweared the juices over the ring muscles of her ass.

"Oh," she gasped with surprise, but she didn't try to stop me.

With gentle, but insistent pressure, I inserted my slick finger, inch by inch, into her tight ass. She moaned, and wriggled against my hand as I worked my finger in and out of her. With my finger fucking her ass, I thrust my cock deep inside her, filling her up in one long thrust.

She cried out with ecstasy.

I fucked her in long, slow strokes, pushing myself deep and hard inside of her, filling her with my cock and finger over and over again. I grasped her hips with my spare hand and pulled her back against me, grinding myself deep into her… she arched her back and moved with me, matching my pace.

I loved this. I couldn't get enough. She'd just come here, dumping whatever else she'd had planned for the day, to run down to my office and offer herself up to me like this… if that didn't make her the perfect wife, then I had no idea what did.

I fucked her frantically, feeling my body begin to arch towards the release I had been craving so intently since I woke up this morning. It was strange. In the past when I was in this kind of mood, I would call up a willing woman from my little black book, hook up with her, and get it out of my system. But I knew, clear as anything, that it wouldn't work like that as long as I was with Willow.

I was addicted to her. Only she would do for me. That itch wouldn't have been scratched until I had her just like this, until I'd filled her and watched her face contort as she—

"I'm coming," she cried out.

Her pussy clenched hard around my cock. The sudden sensation of her body giving in to mine was all I needed to push me over the edge. In time with her, I found my own release, my body exploding with pleasure as I held myself deep inside her.

Trembling, she practically crashed forward on to the desk, her mouth opening and closing as she tried to find the words to speak in the face of what we had just done.

I ran my fingers over her neck, her shoulders, her back, watching as she shivered beneath my touch. Would I ever grow tired of this?

I couldn't see a way I ever could...

I withdrew from her slowly, reluctantly, not wanting to have to send her away and get back to work, but knowing I had no choice.

"I can't... I've never done something like that before..." she whispered when she regained the power of her voice

I pulled my finger out of her ass, cleaned it, and sliding around to my seat, I pulled her onto my lap, letting her plant herself there, so she could catch her breath. Leaning in, I nuzzled my nose into her neck and inhaled the intoxicatingly sweet scent of her arousal.

"Do you have to get back to work now?" she purred in my ear, as she ground her pussy on my slowly hardening dick.

"Jesus, I can't get enough of you," I growled.

She giggled. "And you haven't punished me yet."

"No, I haven't, have I?" I said wryly.

She turned her head so she could kiss me and I got the feeling that it would. indeed, be awhile before I got back to work.

CHAPTER 18

WILLOW

I'd just climbed out of the bathtub when I heard the doorbell ring. The housekeeper and cleaner had just left and I had been looking forward to a relaxing day by myself. With a sigh, I headed over to check who it was. I felt my stomach drop when I saw it was Austin, Gabe's cousin on the screen.

He stared straight into the camera.

I drew back. I knew that he knew I was in and I didn't want to give him the impression I was afraid of him.

Thank God for these video screens.

I headed over to the intercom, glad I would have an excuse to simply brush him off. Gabe wasn't around this afternoon, and I felt sure Austin just wanted to bust in and spend another few minutes trying to guilt him about some contract or other. Pressing the button, I spoke into the speaker. "Hi, Austin. Gabe's not here at the moment, but he's probably going to be back in a couple of hours if you want to—"

"Willow?"

"Yeah," I replied, a little thrown by the confidence and certainty in his voice.

"It's actually you that I want to talk to," he said looking up into the camera above the door. His eyes seemed to cut straight through mine and I felt a shiver run down my spine. I didn't like where this was going, but it wasn't like I could pretend I wasn't in now since I had answered the phone. I just had to suck it up and deal with it. "I'm just out of the shower, I need to get dressed," I explained, trying to keep my voice firm.

"No worries I'll come up and wait for you by the front door," he replied quickly and more firmly than I had sounded.

"Right. Give me a minute." I let go of the intercom button.

Cursing and swearing, I buzzed him in. I should have been able to find a way out of it. I should have–hell, I should have been able to brush him off or something, but I just didn't know how I was meant to get him out of here. He was supposed to be family now, at least in theory...

I got dressed quickly, throwing on some jeans and an old comfortable shirt, then pulling my hair up in a style that kept it out of my face. Taking a deep breath, I gathered myself as best I could before I opened the door to him. I'd felt a hell of a lot safer confronting him when Gabe had been there by my side to support me. In fact, I always felt safer when he was around.

"Come in," I invited, hoping he couldn't read the panic in my voice.

He narrowed his eyes at me and brushed past me over the threshold, into the apartment.

I followed him into the sitting room. He seemed very confident. He behaved as if he owned the place. I watched him walk up to the black sofa where Gabe and I had sex last night and sit down.

"Willow. That's a really unique name, you know that? Not many people in this city are called Willow."

"Yeah?" I murmured, shifting from foot to foot nervously as I waited for him to get to his point. It was obvious he had one and he was taking his time to get to it.

"So it made it pretty easy to do some research on you," he continued in a totally friendly voice.

I frowned.

"See, I thought you must have been another one of the bimbos in his little black book."

Something in my expression made him grin. "Didn't know about that did you? Well, Gabe has this little address book. He's too lazy to date so when he gets horny, he calls one of them and they come over and fuck."

"I hope you have a point."

"Yeah, I have a point. Anyway, I thought the slippery bastard had conned one of them into marrying him to steal the business from under me, but one look at you and I knew a girl like you would never be in his book." He made a vague movement with his hand. "Wrong shape, not enough hair bleach, and too many brain cells. The two of you don't really move in the same circles, now, do you?"

"I don't know what you're talking about," I replied, pulling myself up to my full height and sliding my eyes away from his. "We met, we fell in love. Sure, it was quick, but when you know, you know."

"I wouldn't know," he replied, coolly. "All I know is that the two of you lived pretty different lives until he goes to see my grandfather's solicitor and hears about the marriage stipulation... you do know about that, don't you?" He looked me up and down.

I felt a heat begin to run up my cheeks. I didn't want him to think he was unsettling me, that he was right about this, but he was onto me. "Look, I don't know what you are getting at, but I suggest you stop right now. If you think Gabe has done something wrong, take it up with him. Now get out of my apartment."

"You worked as a waitress before this, I believe?" he continued as if I hadn't spoken. "Not making a lot of money, from what I could see. Lived in a bad end of town with a roommate..."

"How dare you invade my privacy!"

"You'd be amazed at all the information that's out there on public record," he replied coolly. "It's not hard to find out a whole lot about anyone these days. A whole lot that says to me you had pretty good motivation for wanting to accept an offer of marriage from someone in Gabe's position..."

"If you're calling me a gold-digger—"

"Hey, I didn't say that, you did," he replied, smirking infuriatingly.

I clenched my fists at my sides.

He gestured up and down the outfit I was wearing. "I'm just saying, take a look at you," he remarked. "I don't know if you've ever met any of the women Gabe has been with before, but you're not exactly... you're pretty far out of his mold, let's put it like that."

"There's a lot more to Gabe than you know," I countered, furious now.

"Willow, I've known him my whole life," he replied condescendingly. "I know him better than almost anyone, certainly better than some chick who spread her legs for a payout. There's a name for women who engage in that activity..."

"I'm going to ask you one last time to leave," I replied, biting back my fury. I wanted to punch him in the face, and kick him out the door. He was far too close to the truth for my liking and I didn't want to have to defend myself any further than I already had.

"I'm just trying to give you some fair warning," he explained, as though he was doing me a huge favor. "Gabe's... well, I don't want to say slumming it, but..." He gestured at my outfit again.

I had just quickly thrown on what was comfortable and now, I felt distinctly uncomfortable knowing he was looking at me and seeing some half-assed wreck of a woman. These were just the clothes I had worn almost every day when I'd been living back in my real life, but they weren't anything close to what was expected now that I was married to a man of Gabe's stature. "If you really think he's slumming it with me," I replied, trying to keep my head. "Then you should go speak to him about that. It's not my concern."

"So you're really saying that the two of you are just crazy in love?" he sneered.

I clenched my fists tighter, my nails digging into the palms of my hands. If I could have gotten away with slapping him right then, I would have, but I knew he would have just taken that as his point proven or worse, he might hit me back. Besides the last thing I wanted, was to give him the satisfaction of knowing he'd gotten under my skin.

The contract I'd signed with Gabe meant I only had to stick by him as his wife for as long as it took to get the business signed over to him. It didn't mention anything about launching myself at his asshole of a cousin over some shitty implications he was making. No, he wasn't going to get me to lose my cool. All he had were suspicions and allegations. If he'd hoped to get me to confirm them, he had gone about it the wrong way.

"Yes, I am," I replied and gestured to the door. "I think you should leave. Gabe will be back later, and I'm sure he'll be very interested to hear everything you've had to say to me..."

Austin's face dropped and I knew I had made my point. He might have felt bold enough to come here, stand in front of me and say all this to my face, but there was no way in hell, he would do it all in front of Gabe. Gabe wouldn't stand for it. I had to, because I was the woman and I had no choice but to play the demure wife who didn't want to cause trouble.

"Fine," he snapped. Turning on his heel, he marched out of the room. "I'll see you later. But just know... I'm watching you. Closely. I have a feeling this charade won't last too long. Gabe never was one to stick to one woman, especially not a low-class slut like you."

"I think you should focus on your own life for a change," I suggested curtly, not caring how rude I came off now. He deserved it. This guy had walked into my house and basically told me that my marriage was a sham. Sure, he was right, but that didn't mean what he was doing wasn't way out of line.

"And I think you should keep an eye on that husband of yours," he replied as he headed for the door. "Because he is one slippery customer. Past history is a good indicator of future behavior. He'll do to you what he did to me. Cheat you out of whatever he promised you."

"Goodbye, Austin," I replied tiredly. I opened the door for him and hustled him out of the apartment. As soon as I was alone again, I felt my body sag. Yes, I had pretended to be very strong in front of Austin, but his words were swirling around in my brain. Round and round. Confusing me and making me feel insecure and afraid.

Was he right?

Was Gabe really slumming it with me?

Did he tire of women easily?

Would he start sleeping around while I waited for him here alone?

The world I'd lived in before I met Gabe was so far removed from this one that it almost felt as though the two of them couldn't exist in the same city, at the same time. Yet, they did and they do now. My reality and his reality, all wrapped up together.

But for how long?

It was at that moment when I had to accept a simple fact— I was beginning to really fall for this guy. I knew the last thing

I needed was to let my heart get broken by a dude who couldn't have been more upfront about what he wanted from me, but I couldn't help the way I felt. There wasn't a thing I could do to change the way I felt about him. How foolish would I feel if I took the money and spent the rest of my life mooning pathetically over this man?

Having said this, neither of us could deny the fact that there was chemistry there, *serious* chemistry. We had something that burned bright, strong and intense, more intense than anything I'd shared with anyone else before.

When we came together, it felt like the ground was moving beneath us, tectonic plates sliding out of place, earthquakes rocking the two worlds we both inhabited. Something existed there, no matter if it was a contract that brought us together, no matter if Austin had begun to figure out our dirty little secret. I knew I would be with him with or without a contact. Even if there were no money involved.

The problem was... would he choose to be with me if he didn't have to fulfill the terms of his grandfather's will?

CHAPTER 19

GABE

"Are you sure about this?" Willow asked again nervously, as she leaned against the limo waiting to take us to the airport.

"For the last time, I'm certain." I took her hand and squeezed it. "I *want* you there. Besides, you're my wife. It would be pretty weird if you just skipped out on this, huh?"

"I guess so," she agreed and managed a smile.

She'd been a little off the last few days, as though something was bothering her, but I hadn't for the life of me been able to get it out of her. I figured she would tell me in her own time, and in the meantime, the best I could do was make sure she had a great time on this trip we were taking together.

It was a business trip out of the state, heading out to a conference on the other side of the country, normally the kind of thing I would have been bored out of my mind by. But the thought of taking her on our very first trip was incredibly exciting, and I was already running through all the ways we could have a very different kind of fun.

The sex had been incredible from the start, maybe because we knew how taboo it was to go down that path, but it had only gotten better and better with every passing day. We learned to explore one another's bodies, learned the intricacies of what turned us on, and what made it impossible to resist one another.

Hell, I could hardly keep my hands off her whenever we were at home alone together. Then every time we went out, I was bursting in my pants on the ride home. I felt pretty sure some of the staff were beginning to catch on to what was happening, but it was hard to give a damn when I was having such a good time playing with my dear wife in such thrilling ways.

In fact, sometimes I thought being married switched up the intensity between us. It was one thing to have dirty, desperate sex with Willow. It was quite another to know I was doing it with my wife. *My wife.* The man who'd never given getting married a moment's thought. When she tipped her head back on top of me as she came, her hands planted on my chest, her ring would glint in the light, and I would smile to myself knowing that was my brand.

She was mine.

I'd made sure Tina had called ahead to make sure the room we were getting in the hotel was up to my standards. I wanted Willow to have the best of everything. I found myself thrilled at the thought of being able to share my world with her. Most of the women I'd been with moved in this kind of lifestyle and acted in a blasé way to show their sophistication, but it seemed like every corner I turned with Willow was a revelation to her.

Most of the time she could hardly believe what she was seeing.

"So, how long is the flight?" Willow asked as the car pulled away.

"No more than few hours, but it really won't feel like that at all, I promise."

"I've never flown anywhere before," she blurted out suddenly.

I raised my eyebrows at her. "Really?"

"Really," she admitted. "I'm a bit nervous about it, actually. I know you must fly everywhere all the time, but the thought of being that far up in the sky..."

"Don't worry," I murmured wickedly. "I'll make sure to find a way to distract you."

She grinned and snuggled into me gratefully.

I wondered if I should break the news to her now. No, I would wait until we were there, until I could show her what I was talking about in person. She would love it, I was sure.

I almost couldn't wait to see her expression.

We arrived at the airport and the car cut straight through the parking lot then headed around the back, onto the private airstrip.

She glanced over at me, clearly more than a little confused. "What's going on? Aren't we going to the airport?"

I pointed across the tarmac to a small, compact private jet. "That's for us."

"You have a private plane?" she gasped, stunned.

I nodded. "I don't use it as much as I should, but, yeah, I do."

"Wow!" she said slowly, then clapped her hand over her mouth and shook her head.

"What is it?"

Her beautiful eyes turned misty. "Nothing. It's just...I never could have imagined this kind of life for me. Not in a million years. I was born addicted to heroin. My mother didn't want me, and for all of my childhood, I was shunted from foster home to foster home. Nothing bad happened to me. Nobody abused me or acted inappropriately, but I was ignored. I was an ugly little thing, you see. Nobody loved me. All I was given were my basic needs, then I was left to my own devices. The only thing that made my life worth living was my books. And the fact that you can just... that you can just sweep me out of here and take me on an adventure like this... I don't think I'll ever be able to tell you how much it means to me."

I leaned forward and planted a soft kiss on her lips. My heart broke to think of her unloved and moving through the uncaring foster system. I decided right there and then that I would do everything in my power to make her happy. Even if it didn't work out between us, I would make sure she was set up for life. "You know what makes me feel good?"

She shook her head.

"When I see you happy because of something I've done. That's what makes me happy."

"Oh, Gabe," she whispered tearfully.

I knew I was pushing things, pushing things towards an intimacy that went far over the bounds of the contract we had agreed upon, but I didn't care. I just wanted her to be happy. Knowing she was would make this entire trip worth it.

"Let's go," I said, getting out of the car onto the breezy airstrip and helping her out. While my driver was taking our bags out, I led her to the steps to the waiting aircraft.

She hesitated for a moment at the bottom.

I glanced around at her. "Still feeling nervous?"

She nodded, biting her lip. "I'm sorry, I know it'll be fine, and I'm just being a big baby, but I'm just a little freaked out."

"I'm here, okay," I said as pulled her up the steps with me. "Let's sit down and get something to drink. Then you can speak to the pilot, if you want. Or anyone onboard. They'll explain everything that's going on to you, so you'll under- stand what's happening totally and completely."

"Thank you." She sighed, smiling and nuzzling into me.

I guided her inside the door, where an attractive air hostess with a wide smile was waiting for us.

"Nice to see you again, sir," she greeted. I tried to rack my brains to remember her, but I came up blank. I guess I must have flown with her at some point.

"Hello, Mrs. Grayson," she continued, nodding to Willow, who smiled back at her.

"Could you bring us some champagne, please?"

"Of course, sir," she replied, and backed off to take care of my request.

Willow bit her lip, clearly keeping a giggle in.

"What is it?" I asked, nudging her.

She shook her head. "It's just so weird having people behaving as if I was something special, running around doing stuff for me. I was the one doing that stuff for others until not so recently."

"And now you're the one who gets to call the shots," I finished for her.

She beamed at me. "I have to be careful; I might get used to this."

I laughed. "I hope you do," I replied. "Any wife of mine is going to be pampered as hell."

"I should hope so," she replied, putting on a faux-haughty air. "Only the best will do for me."

"And only the best is what you will get," I promised. I knew we were just playing, but I meant it. I wanted to shower her with everything I could, anything that would get that beautiful smile beaming on her face.

CHAPTER 20

GABE

We took our seats opposite each other, then Willow settled down and peered out of the window to the runway outside. The weather was supposed to be good so it wouldn't be long before we took off.

"How much does it cost to run something like this?" she asked, glancing around, her eyes wide.

"I'm not sure exactly how much," I confessed. "I have accountants who take care of things like that."

"I should see if they do a discount private-jet service for waitresses," she joked. "I don't think I'll want to travel any other way from now on."

"What? You'll take the private jet down to the corner store to pick up bread?" I teased.

She laughed. "Yeah, damn straight I will, or I'll get one of my many slaves to bring it to my bed."

"It can work however you want it to work, baby. The world is your oyster."

She caught her breath, as though my words had taken her off-guard.

The air hostess returned with our glasses of champagne, breaking the sudden stillness that had descended between us. I wished I could figure out what the hell was going on inside her head, because something had wormed its way up there and I wanted to know what it was. It seemed like she was holding back something from me. Something crowded between us that hadn't been there before.

The air hostess walked away.

"To us," I toasted. Lifting my glass, I tapped it against hers.

"To us," she echoed and took a tiny sip of the bubbly in the crystal flute before her. Then she was peering out of the window once more.

"You feeling any less nervous?"

She shook her head. "I'm sure I'll be okay once we're actually up in the air. Or I'll panic and jump out of the plane in a parachute, and just walk to the conference."

"Over my dead body you're jumping out of this plane," I growled. It was meant to be a joke, but the thought of her getting hurt made my insides burn like lava.

"Gabe, I'm sorry. I'm being so unsophisticated and childish. Once the plane gets in the air, I'll be better. I promise."

I squeezed her knee. "Hey, it's alright to be freaked out. Really. Doing something new can be scary if you've never done it before. If there's anything I can do to make it easier..."

"Ha, ha, just keep the champagne coming? If I can get

blackout drunk then I don't have to remember any of this anxiety, right?"

I laughed. "Trust me, jet lag and a hangover aren't a good partnership."

"It's my first time flying," she shot back playfully. "Let me be the judge of that, yeah?"

"Sure thing," I conceded. "But don't say I didn't warn you when you have to go through the whole first day wearing dark glasses and trying not to catch anyone's eye..."

"I won't," she promised, and the plane began to move. Her jaw tightened. Despite all the nervous attempts at humor, it seemed clear she was still seriously uncomfortable.

I touched her knee once more and drew her attention back to me. "It'll be fine," I promised her. "Really, I've flown on this thing hundreds of times. I promise you, I only hire the best. They know what they're doing, you are completely safe."

"Well, yeah, but you can't say anything else, can you?" she quipped, trying to keep her tone light. "You can't say 'actually, yeah, this is really dangerous and loads of planes crash.' We could drop out of the sky at any moment..."

We took our final run-up, the wheels churning below us. Her face went pale and I slipped into the seat next to her, putting an arm around her shoulders and pulling her close. "You're going to be all right," I comforted.

Willow nodded, even though she didn't look like she meant it. "Yeah, I am. I trust you. Millions wouldn't, but I do."

I grinned. "That's my girl."

Gritting her teeth, she turned away from me to look outside

of the window. We had just lifted off and Chicago was below us. "Jesus, how high are we going to go? It's a long, long way to the ground." Her head whirled around. "Oh my God, what was that sound? Was it the engine?"

"Relax, it's nothing. It's like driving a car. You use one gear to accelerate and another to cruise."

She turned back to the window restlessly.

I touched her cheek and brought her face back around to me. I needed her to focus on something else. Gently, I kissed her. She moaned softly against my mouth and I knew exactly what I needed to do to keep her from getting too freaked out. She was wearing a short pencil skirt, the very epitome of professional and the sight of her curvy body poured into the tight fabric was turning me on a ridiculous amount. I slipped down in front of her, and pushed her legs apart to expose her panties.

"Hey, hey, what are you doing? What if someone comes in—"

"Don't worry, we're not going to be disturbed," I promised, as I pushed her skirt further up her thighs.

"Don't they come in to serve tea and coffee and stuff?" she said, staring at the closed door.

"Not while this light is on," I explained, pointing to the light I had the designers install in the plane. In the past, I had used it when I wanted to concentrate on work and not be disturbed, but today… I had a totally different use for it.

I brushed my lips over the inside of her thigh. She moaned and tipped her head back, reaching down to run her fingers over my scalp. The air was rushing by the windows, but she didn't seem to give a damn about it anymore.

I moved my mouth further and further up along her thighs, pushing them slowly further and further apart until she was completely exposed to me right there in the middle of the plane. I leaned forward and planted a kiss on her soaking panties, letting my warm breath blow on her pussy through the fabric.

She groaned and wriggled on the seat.

I inhaled the sweet, musky scent of her wet pussy.

I couldn't count how many times I had gone down on her in the last month or so, but every time I did, I just became more and more addicted to her taste and scent. I wanted as much as I could get from her.

I hooked my fingers around her panties and pulled them aside so I could access her sweet little pussy. Pressing my mouth on her clit, I sucked softly on her. Some air hostesses could have walked in even when the *Do Not Disturb* light was on and caught us at any moment, but I didn't care. Hell, maybe some part of me thought that was hot in itself. I wanted the whole world to know just how into this woman I was. I wanted everyone to know Gabe Grayson couldn't get enough of the once-abandoned child nobody really wanted.

"Ah..." Willow moaned softly, lifting her hips and pushing back against my mouth.

Her sweet scent was filling my head and the flavor of her was rich on my tongue, like a fine wine. No woman I'd ever had tasted like her. How could she alone taste so good? As if she'd been made for me, made to match my hunger. Her silky-soft pussy was easily the most delicious thing I'd ever tasted in my life

"Mmm." Her hips ground restlessly against my face. One hand was clamped on the seat next to her and the other had reached down to grasp my head and pull me closer to her as though she couldn't get enough.

I knew she wanted me, truly and deeply, the same way I wanted her. The chemistry we had couldn't be faked or written into being with legal jargon or be bought even with a million dollars. What we felt was as real as the sky around us, as concrete as the earth we'd just taken off from...

The excitement of doing it on a plane made her come quickly, her body arching off the seat as her clit pulsed frantically beneath my tongue. I held my mouth where it was, not quite ready to give up yet, but when she pushed my head away desperately... I relented. She pulled me up on top of her and kissed me deeply, wrapping her arms around me, holding me close. Her breath was coming quickly and her heart was hammering in her chest.

I knew, like me, that she couldn't get enough of this thing between us.

"Fuck me," she breathed in my ear, but before I could do as she asked, a sound drew our attention. I glanced around and saw the air hostess coming back in. I jumped off my wife.

Willow swiftly pulled her skirt down and rearranged herself, her cheeks still adorably flushed from being caught in the act. She bit her lip and glanced at me.

I turned my attention to the hostess.

"Just came to check if you needed anything, sir."

"I think we're doing just fine," I answered and pointed to the sign.

She turned bright red. "Oh, I'm so sorry. I didn't see it. I'll leave you to it," she replied, and ducked out of the cabin quickly.

Willow laughed. "Okay, so I think we have to keep it in our pants for a while yet."

"Maybe for the time being," I agreed. "But are you feeling a little better now? A little less stressed?"

"Actually, I am." She nodded as she looked out the window, where we had just broken the cloud cover and made it into the sky beyond. It was blue as far as the eye could see, and she beamed at the beautiful color. "This is amazing, Gabe," she cried excitedly. Just like a child, she had forgotten her earlier fears.

I watched with the indulgence of a parent. Poor thing, she hadn't had a good childhood. Well, I intended to make it up to her. I took her hand and brought it to my lips. "Anything for my wife."

Willow beamed an angelic smile in my direction.

I wasn't even sure if I was joking any longer.

CHAPTER 21

WILLOW

"So, which way is it to our room?" I asked Gabe as he swept me into the elevator.

He pressed the button on the gold panel. "We're in the penthouse suite."

I laughed. "Of course, we are. You have no idea how the other 99.9 percent live, do you?"

"Of course, I do," he replied. "But I work very, very hard for my money and it's my first trip with my wife, so I'm not making any sacrifices."

"So… we could call this our honeymoon?" I wondered aloud.

He grinned wolfishly. "We could."

The doors swished open smoothly and he led me across a thickly carpeted corridor towards a grand doorway. He swiped his key against the lock and the door clicked open.

After he pushed it open, he held it for me while I entered. I gasped at the sheer luxury and decadence of the vast, high-ceilinged suite. It was so beautiful a shiver went through me. I walked to the middle of the room and looked around me in sheer wonder.

The truth was... no matter how hard I tried, I hadn't been able to get what Austin said out of my head. Was he right? Was I just a novelty? Was Gabe just doing all this because he was slumming it while knowing that he would be able to shake loose of me as soon as he got what he wanted? I felt pretty sure that Austin hadn't confronted his cousin about his suspicions. Instead, he had very cunningly placed them in my head, knowing they would stew in there.

He must have been hoping I would crack and run away with my tail between my legs.

I hadn't told Gabe about what had happened. I told myself it was because Austin's opinion wasn't important to me and I didn't want to give it any more value than it had, but if I were honest, I didn't tell Gabe because I didn't want him finding out and maybe even realizing that he agreed with his cousin.

No matter how much I told myself I didn't care what Austin had said, he'd changed my relationship with Gabe. Now I felt torn about how to react to all the wonderful things Gabe was showing me. I no longer felt like showing him how truly thrilled I was to see or do something I'd never seen or done before I met him. Slowly, but surely, I was stopping myself from showing my excitement because I didn't want to be *that* woman from the slums that he was fucking for a little while.

I couldn't help thinking about what Lorraine said to me either. About getting hurt. Maybe she had a point. Maybe I should have done a better job protecting myself from all of this. Being with him was intoxicating, not just because of the money, the luxury, the excess, and the sex...which was exciting, and better than anything I'd ever experienced before.

If I let myself get used to any of it I would be setting myself up for a fall when the contract ended.

"What do you think?" he asked, approaching me and winding his arms around my waist.

I kept looking down at the city below. I'd never been this far from Chicago before and I was suddenly very aware of how distant I was from everything I'd always known as home. I couldn't even call up Lorraine and ask her to come see me. "It's beautiful," I whispered, but my voice sounded far away and distant.

For a long second Gabe didn't move at all, then he stepped away from me and wandered over to the bar. "Do you want a drink?"

"No, I think I'm okay," I answered, glancing over at him. He was so good-looking he made a crowd of butterflies take off in my stomach. The line between playing his wife and actually just being his wife was starting to get thinner and thinner, and I had to find some way to expand it again. "Maybe I should get some sleep. It was a long journey out here and I could use some time to catch up."

"Sure thing," he replied easily, but he stared at me, as if thrown by the hasty retreat I was beating. "I'll wake you up before dinner."

"Sure." I backed into the bedroom and closed the door behind me. I wasn't tired. In fact, I felt like my heart was breaking. I knew I needed to get a hold of myself, I just didn't know how.

I closed my eyes and rubbed my hands over my face. Then I crashed on the huge bed below me gratefully. I could do this. I could do this for me and Lorraine. I promised her half the money and I couldn't just walk out now. I gave my word to Gabe too. He had kept to his side of the bargain. He didn't deserve to lose because I was silly enough to go and fall in love with him. I was hired to pretend. I could pretend, couldn't I?

As I lay on the bed, I found a strange tiredness catching up with me. My brain was overworked. I closed my eyes. *I'll sleep for a little while.* When I wake up, things would be clearer, better. I would be fresher and I could handle it then.

I jolted awake as soon as the door opened. I thought it'd only been a few minutes, but it was getting darker outside. I pushed myself up at once. "What time is it?" I asked, running my fingers through my hair.

"It's coming up for dinnertime," Gabe replied softly. He sat on the edge of the bed and laid a hand on my leg through the covers.

I withdrew it quickly. It felt as though his fingers were burning through the covers, branding my skin. The light was behind him so I couldn't see his face properly, but I felt him frown.

"They have an introductory dinner in about an hour down-stairs," he explained. "Are you still tired or do you think you'll be able to join me?"

"Well, it would be pretty weird if I didn't, wouldn't it?" I replied. "I'm your wife, after all."

"Yes, you are my wife," he agreed slowly. He watched as I

climbed out of bed and went through the bags I had packed to come out here. "You okay, Willow?" he asked.

The sound of my name called so softly from his lips was more than I could take. I closed my eyes and tried to stem the rush of desire that consumed me in that second. "I'm fine," I replied. "I just need to get ready, that's all."

"I can take a hint," he replied, climbing off the bed, he headed out of the bedroom. "Just come out when you're ready, okay?"

"Okay," I mumbled.

I went through the clothes I'd brought and decided I was going to make sure everyone who saw me would know, from a single glance, that I was his wife. I wanted to match up to him and make him proud to have me on his arm. I was hired to do a job and I would do it to the best of my ability. There wasn't a chance in hell that I was going to let anyone else look at me the way Austin had when he'd accused me of bringing Gabe down to my level of slum.

I'd discovered it was easy to look good when you were buying outrageously expensive clothes that had been designed by masters of their art using the best material money can buy. I stepped into a simple dove gray dress that had cost four months of my old salary and a pair of tan heels. Then I hung long droplets of gleaming diamonds from my ears. A slick of red lipstick finished off the look.

When I went out to meet Gabe, his eyes widened with surprise. "You look incredible."

I slipped my arm through his. I felt suited to him when I was dressed like this. I had my mask on and I could play the part just as well as him. "Shall we?"

He nodded and smiled.

I felt myself start to loosen up a little. Maybe it really had just been the jet lag throwing me off.

We headed downstairs to a private dining room to find a long table filled with a couple of dozen people. They all sprang to their feet when they saw Gabe approaching.

I couldn't help the way my heart swelled with pride to be on his arm, to be seen with him.

He shook hands with everyone, smiling and nodding, greeting his investors and the various people he worked with across the country. He'd tried to fill me in on who everyone was before we'd come out, but I knew I would just have to keep my conversation to a minimum and hope I didn't call someone by the wrong name.

"And this must be the lovely wife we've heard so much about!" an older man exclaimed as he turned his attention to me.

I smiled and extended my hand. "I'm Willow."

He raised his eyebrows. "Willow, huh?" he remarked. "That's an interesting name."

He was just being charming, but it reminded me of what Austin had said and I felt myself flush slightly.

Gabe put his arm around my waist and pulled me in close. "Not the only interesting thing about her, let me tell you," he said with a smile. He was smooth, but not aggressive, defending me without having to come out and stand out there to defend me.

The man raised his eyebrows even higher. "I can imagine." His gaze swept over my body, making me shift uncomfortably.

"So, you're the woman who's managed to get Gabe to settle down," a woman cut in, probably sensing my discomfort.

I smiled at her and nodded.

"Never thought I would see the day," she remarked, glancing between the two of us. "It's great to see you settled down, Gabe. I know it's what your grandfather would have wanted."

"I'm sure it is," he replied and pulled out a seat for me to join them at the table.

Everyone else sat down around us, as though on cue; I felt like we were royalty. A girl could get used to this...

The rest of the evening was much easier than I expected it to be. I'd thought everyone would be pretty much trying to catch me out, the way Austin had, but it seemed like they were just happy Gabe had finally brought a girl along to one of these things. I did pretty well, if I did say so myself. I kept my cool and didn't panic, even when I got asked a few questions about how we met and when we'd decided to get married. I had a couple of glasses of wine and spun the stories with ease. All the while Gabe kept his hand on my thigh beneath the table. I wasn't sure if it was for show, or if it was because he couldn't keep his hands off me.

I wished it were the latter.

By the time we headed back up to the room at the end of the

night, there was a festoon of demands from people for us to visit them soon. Gabe would be at the conference with them for the next couple of days, but they seemed more interested in seeing me again than him.

"They seemed pretty impressed by you," Gabe remarked as we rode up in the elevator.

I raised my eyebrows at him. "You a little jealous?" I felt happy and flirty. All the earlier doubt went with that second glass of wine. I just wanted him, all of him. I had been denied that on the plane by the stewardess walking in on us, and I just wanted to have the best time possible in this beautiful hotel with this beautiful man

He laughed. "Far from it. I'm proud to be seen with you. You must have noticed that you were the hottest woman in that place..."

"Can't say I did," I preened, but the truth was I enjoyed the attention. All my life I'd been the wallflower, sitting unnoticed by myself while everyone else around me danced and laughed. For the first time in my life, I felt bright and attractive.

We tumbled back into the penthouse, the two of us groping each other in our desperation to become one. He pushed me up against the door and kissed me. I was reminded of that encounter we'd had in his office a few weeks ago, when he had called me up there just because he couldn't resist hooking up with me. It had driven me crazy, knowing that he couldn't wait to have me. I'd never had someone want me so deeply, so wildly.

It was intoxicating just to think about, even more so than the wine.

He slid his hand around my waist and pulled me close to him. I felt his hard cock pressing against me. I wanted him inside me, wanted him filling me up, but he seemed to have other plans in mind.

"Come with me," he murmured in my ear. "I have something I want to show you."

"Sounds exciting," I remarked and wobbled slightly in my heels as I followed him into the bedroom.

"I brought something special for us to try," he explained, as guided me on to the bed.

"Something special?" I asked curiously.

CHAPTER 22

WILLOW

He clicked open a bag I hadn't even noticed was there. Out of it, he pulled a small object. It was bulbous at one end and flat on the other, and it had a button on the flat end. Lorraine had one of those and I was thinking about getting one.

"Is that what I think it is?" I asked curiously, my heart already beginning to beat a little faster in my chest. He always knew just how far to push me, exactly what I could take. I trusted him to read me perfectly and I wanted to see what he had in store for me.

"You want me to show you?"

I nodded at once. "I'm pretty sure I could manage that," I replied, already running out of breath. I had no idea how it was going to go, but knew it would be a lot of fun.

"Take off your panties and get on all fours," he ordered.

I did as I was told. I knew what he liked to see so I arched my back and pushed my ass towards him as he moved behind me.

Gabe ran his hand over the small of my back. "You just let me know if this doesn't feel right, okay?" he told me softly.

I didn't care what he was about to do to me. I was already here for it. I heard the squirt of a bottle, and then felt the cool, silky texture of lubricant being rubbed over my pussy... and then up, towards my asshole. "Ah!" I squeaked in surprise. I'd never done anything anal in all my time as a sexually active woman, but not through lack of interest. I'd just had no idea where to start, but luckily, it seemed like the man I was with right now already had a very good idea of what he wanted to do with me.

"I've been thinking about your ass all night long," he murmured, tracing his finger around my puckered, virgin hole and making me squirm with desire and want. How did he always know just what I needed? He eased his finger inside me, and I groaned. He had put his finger into me many times. I guess he was starting the process of stretching me.

"Relax your muscles, baby. You're doing just great," he said as he withdrew his finger.

I felt something larger and fuller pressing against me. I closed my eyes and did my best to relax as he pushed the new toy into me. "Fuck," I gasped as the pain shot through me.

He ran his hand over my ass-cheek, squeezing my flesh. "Shh...just relax. You have the most beautiful ass I've ever seen in my life," he murmured. "You have no idea how much I've wanted to see you like this..."

I groaned again, trying to give shape to the desire pulsing in my system.

"Does it feel good?" he asked.

I managed to nod. I was lost in the sweetness of the feeling, the newness.

"Tell me," he ordered.

I closed my eyes and gathered myself. "It feels... good. Really good," I finally replied.

"Does it make you feel like a dirty girl?"

I turned to look him in the eye. "Yes."

He touched the button on the flat end of the toy, sending it bursting to life in my asshole.

"Fuck!" I cried out. It felt like the sensations were rippling through my body, impossible to stop, to contain. It made my pussy ache for attention, attention he was lavishing on my asshole.

He began to fuck me with the toy, using it slowly inside me, filling me with the bulbous end. I knew it wasn't that big, but it felt huge. I loved it. I couldn't get enough. How had I waited for this long to explore this pleasure? It felt incredible, the sensations spreading through me began to build, build, and build.

"I want to fuck you while the toy is inside you," he murmured.

His words were slicing through my brain. All I could do was nod in agreement, desperate to feel as much as I could. Maybe it was the wine, maybe it was the way his hand had rested on my thigh the whole night through, or maybe it was something else entirely—our chemistry, our desire, always burning bright and impossible to deny. "Yes, I want you to fuck me while the toy is inside me," I gasped.

I heard the rip of a condom packet, then seconds later his cock pressed against my pussy. He rubbed the thick head over my slit for a few seconds before he pushed inside of me.

And just like that, I was double filled.

"Oh..." I groaned, as I tried to make sense of the unfamiliar feelings running through me. I'd never felt anything like it before, the mesh of his cock in my pussy and the vibrating toy in my ass. I couldn't be sure which I liked better, but I knew they matched together. Together, they were unbeatable.

He fucked me slowly, matching his pace to the same one he was using to push that toy deep inside me. The sense of full-ness felt strange and yet wonderful. I wasn't sure I would be able to take it once he started to increase his pace, but he kept at it. Pumping, pumping, pumping into me until I smoothed out onto a wave of pleasure that carried me through any doubt I'd had about whether I would be able to handle it. I was surprised I could keep up with him when it came to stuff like this, but thrilled, too. I loved knowing he had gone to all this effort to please me, to pleasure me, plan-ning in advance to find toys that he knew would push my buttons.

Soon my brain stopped functioning and all I could take in was the way I felt, not just the physical sensation, but the emotional ones, too. A mental side existed to our connection. The way he was taking me, I knew he wanted me, desperately. He was burying himself inside me up to the hilt like he was trying to brand me, make me his forever...

When I came, it felt like the world came crashing in around me. All the doubt I had been nursing about whether or not he was slumming it with me had built into anxiousness, which he had turned into sheer sexual energy with this encounter. The way he built me up slowly, from playing with my ass to fucking me deep and hard, made the orgasm all the more intense. I grasped the bedsheets and buried my face into the pillow to make sure I didn't disturb the rest of the hotel's guests with my scream of pleasure.

He kept moving inside me, pushing the toy deep into my ass like he was wringing the final drops of my pleasure from my body. Finally, I felt him blow his load deep inside my pussy, grinding his hips hard into mine and letting out a shout of triumph as he found his release. My pussy was still clenching around his dick, as though my entire body wasn't ready to give him up quite yet.

Finally, he slowly slipped both his cock and the toy out of me. I collapsed on to the bed, mewling slightly with pleasure. My dress was still wrapped around me, but haphazardly, so he pulled the covers protectively around me.

Gabe retreated out of the room to dispose of the condom, and I stripped out of my dress and stood naked in front of the mirror. My makeup was smeared and my hair looked a mess. Even though I looked ridiculous, I felt incredible.

Utterly sated. Utterly satisfied. Before Gabe, I hadn't been confident about the way I looked, but his ardent worship of my curves left no room for doubt. He thought I was hot as hell, and who was I to deny his truth?

"Admiring yourself?" he asked as he re-entered the room, catching me looking myself in the mirror.

"Maybe..." I would never have been able to say that before I met him.

"Can't say I blame you," he replied as he wrapped his arms around me, tracing his fingers over my hips, my thighs, and the curve of my waist. "This is a pretty impressive package, after all," he remarked, planting a soft kiss on my shoulder.

I smiled and wriggled back against him. I loved the way I felt when I was in his arms. He made me feel protected and adored all at once, a combination I was sure I would never get tired of.

CHAPTER 23

WILLOW

The rest of the trip went by far too quickly for my liking. I wished it could have lasted a little longer, but I knew the time on our relationship was ticking down, constantly, always with a time limit on how long any of this could last.

When we flew home, I peered out the window and wondered if coming back to our real lives was really the best thing for us. I wanted us to fly off to some faraway land, where it was just the two of us and we could pretend this marriage was for real.

Or at least that what we felt for each other went past raw physical attraction.

Because I was sure it did, at least on my side. I was certain what I felt for him was something real, and I wasn't ready to give up on it yet.

"You need a hand?" Gabe asked me as I climbed out of the plane.

I shook my head. It wasn't going to be long before I had to stand on my own again, anyway. The less I learned to rely on him, the better.

Over the next week, I started to feel a little... well, off. It was hard to say exactly what was off about me, but something was wrong, for sure. I frowned at myself in the mirror in the morning, planting my hands on my belly and trying to figure out why I looked so damn bloated. I'd been feeling crummy too, at least in the mornings. Instead of jumping out of bed at the crack of dawn like I usually did, I wanted to just lay in bed and call on the chef to bring me bland food.

At least Gabe was out of the house most of the time, so I didn't have to worry about explaining any of this to him. There was something about the thought of him nursing me while I was sick that felt too intimate, even considering everything we'd done together by this time. Being sick or unwell wasn't at all sexy and I didn't like the thought of sharing the intimacy of my illness with him.

Still, he came in early after work most days to check on me. I would pretend to perk up and we would do things together until I started yawning. I felt disappointed too, because I simply wasn't up to fooling around. I knew the amount of time we had left was swiftly running thin and I was desperate to make the most of the time I still had with this perfect man, but instead, I was constantly lying in bed, feeling tired and slightly depressed.

At first, I wondered if it was to do with the fact that Gabe and I weren't real. Every day that passed brought the big stack of cash closer while it pushed Gabe further away.

After a week of feeling sorry for myself, I decided to head down to the drugstore and collect as much in the way of illness-busters as I could find. Anti-nausea pills, painkillers, anything that I thought might actually take the edge off the worst of what I was feeling. As I wandered down the aisles, my eye fell on a poster for a pregnancy test.

I stared at it.

Oh, God.

Then I started crunching the numbers, trying to remember when I'd gotten my last period. It couldn't be. Surely not, but I decided to pick up a couple of boxes either way. If just for the peace of mind. Nothing more than that.

I headed home and went straight to the bathroom to take the pregnancy test. It'd been thumping in my brain since I had seen the poster and I needed to get it out of my brain before my panicking went any further.

Heading to the bathroom, I did what I had to do, then sat back on the bathroom floor. On the box the test had come in, a couple was jumping up and down, holding each other, their faces set with great grins. They seemed pretty happy about the outcome.

Lucky for them, I guess.

I counted down the seconds in my head, then looked down at the test in my hand. When I saw the result, I nearly tossed it across the room in alarm.

Positive.

It couldn't be.

Oh, shit.

No...

CHAPTER 24

WILLOW

"Are you ready to go?" Gabe called.

I was standing in front of the mirror, twisting this way and that, trying to figure out if there was any kind of baby bump showing. Wondering if this dress did enough to cover it up if there was.

"Yeah, yeah," I called back. "I just need to put on some shoes. I'll be out in a minute..." I quickly put the finishing touches to my makeup. We were headed out to some party thrown by Gabe's company. It was a chance for Gabe to show me off and prove to anyone who was paying attention that we were a happy couple.

Of course, he had no idea about the pregnancy, which was ironic, given I knew he needed an heir to secure the business. He'd told me he was going to take care of it through a surrogate, but thanks to the failure of one of those fancy condoms we had used, I was now carrying the final part of his grandfather's stipulation in my belly.

I didn't know how I was going to tell Gabe. It seemed to me

the thought of an heir was something he'd applied for in theory only... not because he had some deep craving to be a father. Even so, I knew he would have been a good one. He was firm but fair, serious and caring.... all at the same time.

But for the time being, the only thing I had to do was make it through the rest of the night without letting anyone else catch on to the fact that I was pregnant. Until I'd had some time to talk it through with the father of the child, I wanted to keep it to myself. Even though there was nothing I wanted more than to call up Lorraine and blurt out the truth about everything that had been happening.

When I came out, I found Gabe waiting for me outside. He looked so tall and dashing my heart ached for him. I wanted to reach out, touch him, tell him about the baby, but I kept it in. I didn't know how far along he was into his surrogate project, if he even wanted another child. Our child.

Gabe was eating me with his eyes. I swear he looked as if the last thing he wanted to do was go out. "You ready?" Even his voice sounded thick with desire.

I nodded silently.

He moved closer to me, buried his nose in the crook of my neck and inhaled deeply. "God, Willow. Every day you just look more and more beautiful. If ever it could be said a woman was glowing it has to be you. Right now."

I almost winced. As in pregnancy glow?

Outside, the limo waited for us. Gabe opened the door for me to climb in, the perfect gentleman as ever. "Austin's going to be at this thing tonight," he warned as we pulled away from the house. "Stay by my side and avoid him as much as you can."

I felt my belly clench with dread, but I kept my voice light. "You make it sound like he's an assassin out to get me."

"Yeah, well, he might not be an assassin, but there is a lot at stake for him. He wants the company. At the very least, he'll be trying to trick you into proving his suspicions."

I winced. Gabe still didn't know about the time Austin came to the apartment and told me right out that Gabe was slumming it with a girl like me. I could hear the words, loud and clear, still ringing in my head. "Trust me, he's not the kind of guy I'd want to spend any time around," I assured him. "I'll keep well out of his way."

"Good," Gabe replied with a tender smile. "Other than that, just be your normal, charming self. I'm sure they're all going to love you to bits."

When he smiled like that at me, I could almost believe he cared. Really cared. I was more than explosive sex. "Okay," I said softly. As I continued to stare helplessly into his magnetic eyes I became afraid that he would start knowing how I really felt about him so I dragged my eyes away and gazed out the window.

We arrived at the party, and I found myself laying a protective hand on my belly. I already felt protective of the vulnerable little bean in there. It hadn't asked for any of this. It was my job to look after it.

"Gabe, Willow, great to see you," Austin announced loudly as he slimed up beside us.

I dropped my hand from my belly. He would have eagle-eyes

out for anything amiss, and he was the last person I wanted to know about my baby.

"How's it going?," Gabe said, putting his arm around my waist and pulling me close to him.

"Wasn't sure if we'd see you here today," he remarked. "Given, that you were away last week."

"We got back a long time ago," Gabe stated evenly, but there was something different about his voice. "And besides, we're not letting you have all the fun here."

"Of course," Austin replied.

A waiter passed by with a tray of drinks, pausing to offer us something. Gabe ordered a scotch from him, Austin already had a glass of champagne.

I reached out for the same, then remembered I couldn't have anything with alcohol in it. "Do you have anything... alcohol-free?" I asked, lowering my voice.

I could see Austin leaning forward with interest in what I was saying.

The waiter nodded, retreated, and then a moment later re-appeared with Gabe's scotch and my orange juice, but the damage had already been done.

"Not drinking, are we, Willow?" Austin remarked, a strange inflection to his voice. "Strange, you struck me as the type who—"

"Careful," Gabe warned in a cold hard voice I'd never heard before. "Willow is my wife, so watch your mouth."

Austin jerked his head back in surprise. "Hey, I wasn't trying to be rude. You know how much I like my drink."

"Whatever, but you've had your warning. You won't get a second one." Then Gabe took my hand and led me away. When we were a little further away from Austin, he looked down at me. "He's an asshole. Don't pay any attention to him. You were ill all week and if you're not feeling up to drinking booze yet, you just stay with the juice, okay?"

I felt too stunned to reply. I could only nod weakly. My heart felt as if it might burst. The way he had jumped in to protect me. No man had ever done that. I knew then Austin was wrong. He wasn't slumming it with me. We were tied together in some way beyond money and status.

I glanced back and Austin was staring at me with something like hate on his face. I could feel a sinking feeling in my chest already.

Gabe squeezed me tight, obviously sensing my anxiety. "Are you okay?"

I flashed a smile. No matter what, I wasn't going to let him down. I would smile and be the kind of wife he could be proud of.

The rest of the night passed without much difficulty, but the whole time I was there, I could feel Austin watching me like a hawk. Finally, to my great relief, Gabe pulled us out of the party. I let out an audible sigh of relief as soon as we were in the limo, out of sight of Austin and everyone else. I'd never before been under such intense speculation and scrutiny.

"You all right?" Gabe asked me, a frown on his brow.

"Yeah, of course," I replied, but my voice was weak and I knew I wasn't selling anything.

"You didn't drink at all tonight," he pointed out. "Don't you feel well? I can call up the doctor and get him to come right away."

"No, no, I don't need that," I assured him quickly. "I just need —uh, I just need..." I trailed off. I didn't know what to tell him. My unfinished sentence hung in the air between us.

"Need what?"

I sighed. "Time. I just need a bit of time."

The car pulled to a halt outside the house, he helped me out, and we headed up the stairs together.

"What's wrong, Willow?" Gabe asked gently once the door closed behind us.

I bit my lip and stared at him. He would have to find out sooner or later. So it might as well be now. "Okay. There's— there's something I haven't been honest with you about. I mean, I didn't lie or anything. I just haven't told you about it… yet."

He stared at me, silent, strong, prepared for anything.

I took a deep breath, mustered all of my courage, and dropped it on him, "I'm pregnant." It didn't even sound like my voice coming out of my mouth as I spoke those words. Instinctively, I put my hands on my belly as if protecting the little baby I was carrying inside me.

"And it's—it's mine?" he asked in an odd, choked voice.

I nodded quickly. "I haven't been with anyone else for more

than a year. One of the condoms we used must have failed or something, I'm not sure." I knew I was babbling, but I couldn't stop myself. "I promise, I never planned this, I didn't want this to happen. I am sure—"

"Stop, Willow. Stop." He even raised his hand as if all my words were like blows he was fending off. His eyes were shining, as though he was looking into a future he had never imagined before.

"What?" I whispered.

He grinned. "This is... this is good. Very good. Fucking perfect, actually!"

"Perfect?" I echoed.

"Of course, it is," he shouted before throwing his head back and laughing.

Okay, so this was a good sign, I felt pretty sure it was.

"The most important part of the stipulations in that will was that I had to come up with an heir. And now, I have."

"What about the surrogate baby?"

"I got a bit sidetracked by you. I was planning on starting that next week."

"Well, I'm only a couple of weeks gone. It's going to be while before the baby is born."

"I've waited all my life to get the company. What's another nine months?"

"Right, of course," I agreed, but I felt my heart sink. He just saw the baby as the means to land the business once and for all. This wasn't about me, or us, or a family. This was

147

about what it had always been about. Him getting Grayson Inc.

"You have no idea how happy this makes me, Willow," he murmured, as he caught my face in his hands and kissed me. Before I knew it, I was kissing him back. Close to his body like this, I could convince myself this was how it was meant to be. I'd just told the man I was married to that I was pregnant with his child, and now he was holding me, happy, thrilled, elated.

Then he pulled back, and I couldn't pretend anymore. None of it was real. He was my husband, but he wouldn't be for long. The clock was ticking. And the baby inside me wasn't the beginning of a family we would construct together. I felt the backs of my eyes begin to burn and I knew I needed to be away from him for a while. "I need the bathroom," I mumbled, and quickly turned away so he would not see the tears in my eyes.

Even before I had retreated into the safety of my bedroom, tears had begun to flood down my cheeks.

CHAPTER 25

WILLOW

"Oh, my God."

"I know."

"No, but seriously, *oh my God!*" Lorraine stared at me from across the table, her jaw hanging open. She looked like I had just up and landed two giant slaps on either side of her face.

I knew how she felt. My brain was still fizzing over it.

"You're pregnant? You're *really* pregnant?" Lorraine repeated incredulously, leaning forward.

I nodded. "I'm really pregnant." I'd taken at least three more tests to confirm that this wasn't some kind of false reading, and I felt entirely confident I was actually in the family way.

"I can't believe this is happening. What does Gabe think about this whole thing?" she asked. "I mean, you've told him, right?"

"Yeah, he knows. He's happy about it. It means he gets what

he wants, doesn't it? He needed an heir, now I'm pregnant, so he doesn't have to go out of his way to find a surrogate. It's convenient, I guess."

"Yeah, but it's not exactly convenient for you," she shot back, always on my side. "Do you even want this kid? What's going to happen when you have it? Are the two of you going to stay together, or are you just—"

"Honestly, Lorraine, I have no idea what happens next," I confessed. "I just needed to talk to someone about all of this, or else my head was going to explode."

"You know I'm always here for you. And if you need someone to step in and help raise this baby, then you know I'm going to be right there too."

I felt a pain in my chest. "I really appreciate the thought," I said in a choked voice. It was good knowing someone was on my side with all of this. Until I met Lorraine, I had always felt alone in the world. Only after I met her had I felt close to another human being.

"And do you..." she began, then hesitated.

"What is it? If you're going to be my future baby-momma you should be able to tell me anything."

"Do you have feelings for him?" she asked finally.

I paused for a moment, letting her words hang in the air. I would have liked to be able to brush it off and tell her I felt nothing for him, he was nothing more than a great fuck and a quick way to a million dollars, but it would have been a lie. "Yes," I whispered. "Yes, I do."

"Oh, honey," she cried.

I knew it was a sound from her heart. She was suffering for me.

The waiter came over then and we were forced to turn our attention to him and what we were going to order. I was glad to have something to draw my attention away and when he was gone, I told Lorraine I didn't want to talk about Gabe or the baby for a while.

The rest of the meal, we talked of other things. Well, I listened and she tried to draw a laugh out of me. She was good to me, a better friend than I had suspected. I felt so grateful for her existence. I wouldn't have been able to make it through this whole mess without her.

When the meal was over, she gave me a tight hug, pulled back and looked into my eyes. "It's going to be all right, Willow," she promised. "It's going to be okay. I'm here for you. We'll figure this out. Like we always do."

"I know we will," I agreed. I hoped my smile was enough to paper over the cracks I was feeling inside.

She squeezed my shoulder. "You know I love you, right?"

Tears welled up in my eyes. "You know I love you right back, right?"

We hugged again

I could have called for the limo or gotten a cab back, but I decided to walk. I needed to clear my head. The restaurant was only a few blocks away from home. *Home.* It was funny, I had started to think of Gabe's apartment as my home now.

When did that trick of the light happen? The apartment I lived in with Lorraine was my real home and would be again when I returned to it. His home was mine only for now...

And that was when everything went black.

CHAPTER 26

WILLOW

The first thing I noticed was the smell, dank and musty. It filled my head like the scent of a cheap beer spilled on an old floor. The first reaction was nausea. Then fear. Jesus. Where was I? Something, a sack, or a bag made out of rough fabric was pulled over my head. I pressed my lips together to keep from screaming or letting the smell get too deep into my brain.

My hands were bound with thin ties.

And I was tied to a metal chair.

I was someone's prisoner.

Whose?

I tried to piece my fragmented memories together, but I was having trouble getting everything to stick. It had all happened so quickly. I was walking down the street in bright daylight after lunch with Lorraine. Walking almost in a daze. Concentrating on nothing but my thoughts. Not even properly registering the sound of a car screeching to a stop on the street just behind me. Then the sensation of a sharp prick on my arm. As blackness descended with a man's arms wrapping themselves around me from behind.

I'd been kidnapped in broad daylight. Would they be sending a ransom note to Gabe?

I felt remarkably calm given the situation, my brain oddly focused. I didn't scream or move a muscle. I knew if I panicked, nothing good was going to happen. I had to keep my shit together for myself and for my baby. I knew Gabe would pay to get me back. The baby and I were the ticket to him having Grayson Inc.

I tried to figure out my surroundings. It smelled like I was in the basement of some gross old house, the cold damp air sinking into my skin. I tried to pull my hands apart, testing the strength of the ties, but a voice came from behind me.

"I wouldn't bother with that, if I were you."

I recognized it. I heard footsteps making their way around the chair. The bag was pulled away from my head. My jaw dropped when I saw the identity of my kidnapper. "Austin?" I gasped.

His face seemed set a little harder than it had been before, his jaw tense, his body intense with energy. Energy, he had focused on me. "Yes, it's me, Austin," he mocked with a sneer.

"What the hell do you think you're doing?" I demanded, glaring at him.

"I'd be very, very careful how you talk to me if I were you. My big, strong cousin isn't here to protect you and I don't like you, so there's nothing to stop me from kicking the shit out of you."

With fear fluttering in my chest, I peered up at him once more.

"That's better. Now, where was I? Yes, I've done a bit of research and uncovered a few little secrets about you."

"What are you talking about?" I fired back, hoping that my voice was doing a decent job hiding the utter terror pulsing through my system. Until I saw him, I'd been able to convince myself it was a straight-up kidnapping job and all I had to do was stay calm and wait for Gabe to pay them off. But now knowing this monster was the one responsible for snatching me—a man who clearly wished me harm—I knew I was in serious trouble.

"You know exactly what I'm talking about," he replied, voice terse. "Your deal? With Gabe? I knew he would never hook up with someone like you, turns out I was right all along…"

"You don't know what you're talking about," I replied desperately. But I knew it was over. He knew about the deal, he knew about the contract. The best I could do was keep deflecting long enough for someone to notice I was gone and do something about it.

"Oh, drop it already, Willow," he replied, waving his hand with irritation. "I know about the contract between you and Gabe. I know this whole thing is a scam for you to get some cash and for him to steal the company from me."

"He's not stealing the company from you. He worked his whole life for it. He deserves it."

"Is that what he told you? What a little liar he is. My grandfather put that stipulation in because he wanted me to have the company. I was his favorite. He didn't trust your husband

and he was right, wasn't he? He's just a low-down thief. Lusting after what isn't his."

I fell silent. What could I say? I could have announced I was pregnant and hoped it would be enough to earn some decency from him, but I had a feeling revealing that knowledge wouldn't help me at all. It might even make it worse. "How did you find out?" I asked quietly. I had no idea what kind of deranged game plan he'd put together, but I wasn't going to risk getting him angry by continuing to deny his accusations. The only real choice in front of me was to somehow negotiate with him.

"Did a little research on you, saw that you had a roommate before you went for my cousin," he explained proudly, clearly impressed with his own powers of deduction. As though any idiot with enough cash couldn't have figured out the same thing. "And I guessed she might know a little something about whatever the fuck was going on between the two of you," he continued. "So, I found out where she liked to hang, went to a bar, met up with her..."

"You stalked her?" I gasped. The thought of my dear, precious Lorraine being dragged in on all of this made me want to scream.

"I found her at a bar and chatted her up," he replied coolly. "And she was very happy to give me everything I needed to know. She told me about this crazy stroke of good fortune that one of her family had recently received, how she still couldn't believe it, how she couldn't tell anyone about it though, because it was a big, big secret..." he trailed off, smiling at me.

"So, you know now," I snapped. "What do you want from me?"

"I want you to break the contract," he replied.

I pretended to snort and shook my head. "I'm not going to do that. Do you know how much money I'm making from it? Well, that might not seem like a lot to someone like you, but for me—"

"And that's why I want to offer you double the money he did to put an end to this stupid charade," he countered.

I fell silent and pretended to consider this. I knew I shouldn't accept his offer straight away. I needed to drag it out and pretend to be greedy, pretend to be what he thought I was. "No," I stated in a hard, cold voice. "The company is worth far more than that."

He raised his eyebrows at me. He thought he had my number. "How much?" he spat.

"Five million."

"That's a lot of money for a waitress to demand."

"If that's too rich for you, then there's no deal to be had."

He did a strange thing then. He smiled slyly as if he'd been hiding his ace up his sleeve. "I don't think that's an option you want to take."

I shifted on the hard chair nervously. "What do you mean?"

"I meant, if you don't sign my contract, there could be an accident." His voice dripped with menace. "And something real bad could happen to you *and* the baby."

My heart stopped. How in the name of holy hell did he know

about the baby? Now I was truly scared. Before, it had just been me on the line here, but now my baby was in play too. I realized it wasn't me playing with him—it was him playing with me all along. "How did you find out...?" I mumbled, staring at a spot on the ground. My head hurt, my vision was starting to blur around the edges.

"I figured it out when you didn't drink at that party, and from the way you kept touching your belly all night long," he sneered. "Let me guess. Gabe added on a little extra cash for you to leave without the baby after the divorce."

"You don't know what you're talking about!" I yelled. My voice was shaking. I couldn't help myself. I couldn't stay calm and collected. I was too frightened. "We—it's real, we feel something for one another, it's not just the contract—"

"Then I guess you'll want to take care of that baby and sign my contract. The sooner you do it the sooner we can all go back to our little lives," he said silkily.

I stared at him in horror. I knew that even if I signed his contract, the chances of the baby and I getting out alive were nil. There was no way he would allow Gabe's heir to leave this basement alive. I felt a superhuman surge of protective-ness and fury inside my body, one that practically drove me to try and tear the bindings off my wrists, and punch him in the face right then and there.

My entire body felt like it was going to burst. I wanted to hurt him before he could kill my child. I wasn't sure if it was anger or terror pulsing through my veins, but whatever it was, it *burned.* I opened my mouth and with a scream of fury, I tried to rise up and rush at him, but all I did was launch the chair with me into the air. I landed on my side as the chair hit the hard floor with a loud clattering sound. I didn't feel any pain and I took pleasure from the expression of shock and fear I had seen in Austin's face when he saw me fly into the air.

Before either of us could do anything, a commotion sounded at the top of the stairs. I glanced up to see what was happening and my heart twisted in my chest when I saw someone I recognized.

Gabe.

He barreled down the stairs straight towards Austin.

"How the hell did you get here?" Austin demanded, backing away in fear.

Gabe shoved him, hard, and he staggered back a few steps but managed to regain his balance. "You cheap piece of shit! How dare you? Gabe snarled. With that, he landed a blow on Austin's chin. It was so hard the sound seemed to echo and reverberate through the room, making me jump.

Austin crumpled to the ground and Gabe came hurtling towards me.

"Are you okay?" he demanded as he pulled the chair upright, then quickly started to undo the bindings on my wrist.

"I'm—I'm fine, I think," I replied. I'd never seen him so fervent in all the time I had known him and even though it wasn't aimed at me, I still found it a little scary.

"And the baby?" he asked, as he set me free.

I thought of the fall when I'd launched myself at Austin, but I felt no pain or wetness trickling down my thighs. "I think everything is okay."

"Thank God," he whispered as he pressed his head into my stomach, clutching and pulling me in tight.

I buried my face against his hair, inhaling the scent of him. My heart was pounding so fast it felt like it might burst out of my chest.

"The police are on their way," he explained as he guided me to my feet. "We don't need to stick around. My guys will explain everything to them."

"I'm so sorry," I blurted out.

Gabe shook his head and touched my cheek. "You don't have anything to be sorry for," he said and there was so much pain in his voice, I knew he meant it.

CHAPTER 27

GABE

I gathered her gently into my arms and she wound her hands around my neck. She nuzzled in close as I carried her out of the car. I didn't want to be apart from her, not for a moment, not for a second. We didn't speak much in the car. I just kept glancing at her white face, asking her again and again if she was all right, and thanking God I'd been able to find her before anything terrible had happened.

At last, I had her back where she belonged.

"Are you all right?" I asked for the hundredth time as I laid her down on the couch.

"I think so." She nodded. "At least, there's no visible injuries."

Her voice was light, but I could tell she was seriously hurting. She looked exhausted. I couldn't even imagine how she must be feeling. Sure, I had managed to get in there before my bastard cousin had managed to do too much damage to her, but still.

She had been kidnapped, fucking *kidnapped,* right out from under my nose!

I called the doctor and he said he would be at the apartment in an hour. Later that evening, I had arranged for the police to come and get her statement while my lawyer was present, but for now she was all mine.

She yawned, pushed herself upright, and managed a smile.

I sank down onto the couch beside her and wrapped my arms tight around her, holding her close. I couldn't believe how close I'd come to losing her, and the baby. When she'd recounted the part of the encounter where Austin had threatened our kid... I wished I had kicked his head in. The fury I felt was incredible. My gut still burned with it.

"Can I ask you something?" she whispered.

I stroked a strand of hair back from her face and nodded. "Of course, you can. You can ask me anything."

"I was just wondering..." She eyed me curiously. "How did you find me so quickly? How did you know where I was?"

I sighed. I supposed now was as good a time to come out and tell her the truth about it as any.

I pointed to the ring that glistened on her finger like a teardrop. "Hidden between the diamond and the gold back is the smallest GPS tracker in the world. It is connected to a powerful system that can track you anywhere in the country. I put it there to make sure I would never lose track of you," I confessed.

Her eyebrows shot up. "You've been spying on me?"

I lifted my hands in defense. "No, not at all. My lawyer

suggested I should get an app on your phone in case you tried to renege on the contract or something, but I went to the ring," I admitted.

Willow shook her head, laughing in disbelief. "You really thought there was a chance I might do that?"

"Honestly? I didn't know you at that time, so yes," I replied. "But I felt shitty about it, especially once we started living together and I was going to turn it off, but then I saw the way Austin looked at you that day he came to the apartment and something told me not to. As it happened, my instinct was right."

"It sure came in handy today," she said slowly.

"Hey, now that Austin's out of the picture, we don't have to worry about him ever again," I promised her.

"But how did you figure out that I was gone?" she asked, furrowing her brow. "I was meant to be out with Lorraine anyway, didn't you think I was just staying late with her?"

"That's the weird thing about me," I confessed. "I think I've become obsessed with you. Every time you leave the apartment, I start to worry about you. I can't stop calling you. When you didn't answer your phone, I got in touch with the surveillance company immediately to check your location. When you weren't where you said you were going to be and instead were in a seedy neighborhood, I knew something was wrong. I called Austin and when he didn't reply, I figured he must have been involved somehow..."

"You suspected him right away?"

"Every crime is easy to solve when you follow the money," I

growled. "He's always been jealous of me. He couldn't bear it to see me happy with you."

"He didn't seem to think we were close," she murmured, lowering her voice and her gaze. "He thought that you'd just —that you'd just paid me to carry the baby."

I grasped her chin and turned her face towards me. "Hey, you don't believe that, do you?"

She gazed at me for a moment, then shrugged. "I don't know what I believe. You did, after all, pay me for all this—"

"In that case, now that Austin's out of the picture, there's no good reason for me to keep up with the charade, is there?" I pointed out.

"You still need the baby," she continued, obviously still terrified that I would agree with what was coming out of her mouth.

I shrugged. "I told you before how I planned to get my heir. I don't need you for that."

Willow gazed at me, her eyes glistening. "Well, why am I still here then?" Her teeth sank into her lower lip.

I didn't respond right away as my gut clenched at the hurt in her eyes.

"Why don't you just tell me?" she whispered.

"Because I love you."

Her beautiful gray eyes became enormous. "You do?"

"I do. You've changed everything. I didn't think that I could ever want to be a father, until I met you. But the moment you told me you were pregnant, I knew that was what I wanted.

Oh, my God, even the thought of him hurting you or our baby..." I reached out and laid my hand on her stomach. It felt strange to think that a tiny version of us that we had made together was growing inside her.

She laced her fingers through mine and smiled.

I managed to smile back at her. "I'll love you until the day you fall in love with me too. I'll warn you now, I don't ever give up."

"What if I'm already in love with you?" she asked softly.

Her words were like a sunburst in my heart. I wanted to pick her up and throw her into the air, but I knew she was delicate right now. When I had set her down on the couch before, she'd winced, which meant she had bruises on her body.

She leaned up to kiss me and I kissed her back, my woman, my wife, the mother of my child. I tucked my hand behind her head and pulled her in close, teasing her with my tongue. When I pulled back, her eyes were soft and heavy-lidded.

"I think we need to go get you cleaned up," I murmured as I lifted her gently from the couch.

She was so light, I felt as though I could carry her for miles. I liked that. Made me feel like I could protect her, which was my only duty now that Austin had been taken care of. I thought of my child growing inside her and couldn't wait for the day it would make its appearance.

I took her to the bathroom, the first place I'd seen her naked. How my life changed that day. I gently put her down on the edge of the bathtub and opened the taps. While the water cascaded down into the tub, I slowly undressed her, coaxing her clothes off until she was completely naked. Just the way I liked her. But I was right. There were bruises on her left side, on her arms, her hips, and thighs. I would ask her about it later, not now. This time was for us. Scooping her into my arms, I gently lowered her into the warm water.

This was how I'd found her that day. I'll never forget it as long as I live.

She let out a groan of satisfaction and I pulled off my own clothes to join her. I wanted to feel her soft, warm skin against mine, remind myself that this was real... as real as it comes.

"Here," she murmured as she handed me some of the fancy shower gel the housekeeper always set on the edge of the bath.

I squirted some into my hands and rubbed it into a soft lather. Slipping behind her, I massaged it on her skin, moving my hands all over her soft, supple flesh.

"That feels so good," she murmured, turning to face me.

My cock was already hard and this time there was no holding back, no reason to doubt what we had. I adored her, every inch of her and I wanted to prove it. I leaned forward and pressed my lips against hers. Then wrapping my arms around her, I pulled her onto my lap.

There were no bruises around her waist or ribcage so I curled my hands around that area and lifted her onto my erection. She reached down and fisted me as I impaled her on my shaft. It wasn't the first time I was inside her without a condom. We'd been going bare ever since I found out she was pregnant.

But the feeling of our bodies coming together today felt different.

It was almost more than I could take. I loved the way her body moved against mine as she parted her legs and pushed herself down until I was balls deep. The soft, sweet scent of the shower gel floating off her skin tantalized me. It was nearly magical. I ran my hands down her shoulders and kissed the spots my fingers traced.

I thanked God this woman had come into my life.

Willow moved up and down my shaft, then after a while, I stopped noticing where her body started and mine ended. I just felt us joining, completely and utterly, in a union that I had never felt before in my life. I'd fucked plenty of women before, but it had never been like this, never. This was something different, something special. When she turned and looked into my eyes, I felt that jolt of recognition. I'd always loved her. In another life, another timeline, another dimension. Who knew?

This wasn't the first time.

I kissed her deeply, flexing my hips and moving deep inside of her. I felt her ring pressing against the back of my neck as she held me close. Her body was so perfect to me, the home to everything I held dear, her soul, our baby, my heart. She moved faster and time seemed to fall away, replaced by something far greater, far sweeter, something that existed only between the two of us.

When she came, she pressed her face into my neck and bit me.

I felt as though I was absorbing her pleasure. The thought

drove me over the edge and I found my own release deep inside of her. My seed shot into her belly. When she pulled back from me, her eyes were wide, and I knew what she was going to say a second before it came out of her mouth.

"I love you," I murmured at the same time she whispered into my ear.

"I love you, Gabe Grayson."

My heart felt as if it was overflowing. I knew I would have to deal with Austin, eventually, but I didn't mind. Not when this woman, this perfect woman, was mine. "And I'm going to love our baby just as much," I promised her. "Nothing can change that."

Willow leaned down to kiss me once again.

I let myself get lost in the impossible sweetness of her lips and her love.

EPILOGUE

Willow
(Two years later)

"**I** can't believe it's been two whole years since the two of you got married," Ella, one of the guests, sighed, gazing between the two of us like we were a fairytale prince and princess.

"Trust me, I've counted every day," Gabe replied, leaning over to drop a kiss on my cheek.

I smiled and nestled against him… my man, my sweet man. "You mean counting down the seconds till you can get away from me, right?" I teased.

He laughed. "How about I grab us another drink?"

I smiled and nodded. "Just a juice for me," I reminded him. "I want to be sober when I see Jilly tonight."

"Of course," he replied.

I watched fondly as he headed across the room to grab another drink. Ella had been swept away by someone else, and I was glad for a moment of peace amongst all this madness.

The party had been thrown to celebrate a big contract Grayson Inc. had managed to land a couple of weeks before, the first that would turn his business into an international competitor in the food distribution world.

It was odd to think that this place hadn't even belonged to him when we got married, given the way he moved through it with such confidence and popularity. Even just walking across the room, he was being stopped by many people keen to chat him up. Ever since Austin had been arrested and put away, his dominance in this place had been unquestioned.

I dropped my gaze to my phone. I couldn't get my mind off little Jilly. We'd left her at home to come out here. I knew I shouldn't be feeling guilty, given that she was with the loveliest nanny in the city, who'd worked for us ever since my baby was born, but I couldn't stop missing Jilly like crazy whenever she wasn't with me. However, I had to leave her because tonight was the night I wanted to break the news to Gabe. I wasn't sure how much longer I could wait either.

I hid a yawn and smiled as Gabe approached with my drink. Taking a sip, I hoped the sugar would be enough to pep me up.

He smiled and lightly touched my arm. "You getting tired?"

I nodded apologetically. "Yeah, I'm really sorry," I replied, pulling a face. "It's been a busy few weeks, after all."

"Well, I wouldn't have been able to do this without you."

I smiled. I'd become the events manager for the company around a year ago, and I had to say it was the perfect job for me–I enjoyed the organizing, the fun of putting together a party and–of course, slipping Lorraine onto the guest list. This was my favorite part, taking her to all these fancy events. I'm hoping she'll find someone gorgeous and settle down. No luck yet, but I've got my fingers crossed.

She'd always loved the apartment Gabe and I lived in so Gabe gave it to her as a birthday present and set her up with her own business. At first, she didn't want to accept, but all I had to do was ask her if she'd do that for me if she was in my shoes. Since then I have done my best to see that she moves in the right circles to meet a nice guy who will not see her as a meal ticket, but will love her and take care of her the way Gabe does me.

I looked into Gabe's beautiful, waiting eyes. "Does that mean I'm allowed to duck out early?"

"That means that we are," he replied, and his gaze moved slowly down my outfit. "Though with you in that dress, you should be grateful I've even managed to last this long."

"Come on. Let's get out of here, before you do something you shouldn't in front of your investors."

Our driver took us home. Then I practically sprinted up the steps to our house and up towards Jilly's bedroom. We had purchased this place a few months after I'd found out I was pregnant. It was more suited for a family than his impersonal apartment. I'd spent months decorating it in readiness for our baby's arrival.

As I stepped into the nursery, I felt again how perfect everything was. I could hear Gabe saying goodnight to the nanny downstairs as I walked over to the crib to give my daughter a hug. "Hey, baby," I cooed into her ear, as she snuggled sleepily against my body. She was tired, that much was obvious, but there was no way I was going to bed without seeing her. I couldn't get to sleep unless I'd spent at least a few hours of the day with her. Even just being at the party for the evening had been enough to make me ache to hold her.

She was the sweetest thing you ever saw, with her father's eyes and my hair. She had grown up so much already, this tiny creature that Gabe and I had made together. Lorraine called her a little devil, but in truth, she was my angel. Even if she wasn't going to be the only one for much longer.

"Is she okay?" Gabe asked quietly behind me.

I turned to smile at him. "Oh, look how the little minx comes alive when she hears her daddy's voice."

Little Jilly was definitely a daddy's girl. She reached out her hands and grabbed at the air in the direction of her father's voice.

I handed her over to him and she laughed happily.

"Hey, honey," he greeted in that voice he only used with her. It was a mixture of love and tenderness.

She let out a happy little snort.

I watched as Gabe cradled her in his arms and smiled to myself. Now was the perfect time. We were all here, as a family, and it only seemed fair to tell the two of them that there was another member on the way. "Gabe?"

He turned to me with that look on his face he always got when he was around her. "Yes?"

"I'm pregnant."

He stared at me for a second, and then slowly placed Jilly back in her crib.

For a second, I felt sure he hadn't heard me. He jerked his head towards the door and I followed.

"Gabe? Did you hear what I said?" I asked, as we walked through the door.

He turned to me in the corridor, closed the door, and scooped me up into his arms.

I burst out laughing.

He'd heard all right. He was just waiting until we were out of the room so he wouldn't disturb Jilly. "I can't believe this," he murmured against my neck as he put me back on the ground. "This is amazing. How long have you known?"

"This morning," I replied, giggling. "I was going to call you at work, but I wanted to see your face when I told you. Then I didn't want to tell you at the party. I decided to wait for the perfect time."

"Baby, you know there's no such thing as a perfect time when it comes to something like that. Next time, I want to know right after you pee on the stick. Actually, I want to be there when you pee on the stick." He dropped to his knees in front of me and planted a kiss on my stomach, then pressed his ear to it.

I held his head there, laughing at his goofiness. For a man so utterly in control when it came to business, he could be so silly when it came to our children.

"I think I can already hear him in there," he remarked.

"Him?"

"Yeah, well, I think it better be a boy, otherwise I'm going to be overrun by girls. All of whom will have me twisted around their little fingers," he teased. Then he stood up and kissed me again. This time, though, there was more urgency to the feel of his mouth against mine.

I knew he wanted more.

He slipped his hands up and under my dress, pushing the skirt up over my hips so that I was exposed to him. Pushing his fingers over my bare thigh, he drew a groan out from between my lips.

"Maybe we should take this to the bedroom," he suggested, lifting me off the ground and carrying me to the big room we had made our own. He was mine and I was his. We belonged to each other, utterly, and soon we would add to our little family to prove that over again.

Gabe laid me down on the bed and pulled my shoes off, one by one, followed by my dress. I was bare-naked underneath. I moaned softly as he lowered his mouth to my nipples, kissing and sucking softly on the exposed flesh. I slipped my hand down between his legs to touch his cock, that beautiful cock I knew would always be mine.

He was already rock-hard. I remembered the very first time we had sex. It was so distant and obscured by the hundreds and hundreds of other times we'd done it in between, but every detail was still just as vivid. "I need you inside me," I breathed in his ear.

He didn't need me to tell him twice. Pulling down his pants, he fisted his cock and pressed the head against my slit. With one thrust, he was inside of me and all I could do was cry out at the sheer pleasure of feeling my man in me once again. There was nothing like it in the world. His body had been made for mine and I would never get tired of feeling our connection come together like this.

I arched my back from the bed and pushed my hips towards his, groaning loudly when he sank his teeth into my ear like he was trying to take a bite out of me. I knew how he felt. Sometimes, I got that feeling too, an urge to consume him, to make ourselves part of one another. I adored that about him, the way he could read my mind.

Just another reminder of how right he was for me.

I moved my hand down between my legs and began to play with my clit, brushing my fingers softly over my engorged nub in time with his thrusts. When I came, I came hard. My upper body lifted off the bed and I buried my face in his shoulder while tightening my grip on him.

I never wanted to let him go.

My pussy was still pulsating around his cock when I felt him come inside me, filling me with his warm cum. He brushed his mouth over mine one more time and slowly withdrew. Flopping back onto the bed, he turned to look at me. He was still half-dressed so I started to unbutton his shirt. He clasped my hands in his, and drew them to his lips. "You looked so beautiful tonight."

"Must be that pregnancy glow," I joked.

"Or maybe it's just you," he replied as he pulled me close to him.

I snuggled into him and closed my eyes. I always got sleepy after we made love.

"I love you so much," Gabe whispered.

"I love you, too."

And with that, I closed my eyes, pressed myself against him, and started dreaming about what our family would be like after our new addition came along.

The End

Watch out for Lorraine's story…

COMING SOON...

LET'S PRETEND

Chapter One
Scarlett

hat?" I gasped in shock. "It cannot be. He would never do that. I don't believe it. There must be some mistake."

Ernest, my father's solicitor shook his head. "I'm sorry Scarlett. There is no mistake. I drew up this will, your father read, and signed it. This is what he wanted."

"But he wouldn't have left Wotton Hall to," I cried, flinging my hand in the direction where my stepmother was sitting, dressed all in black, as if she truly was mourning. "She hates it. She called it a mausoleum right to his face."

Ernest looked at me sadly. "I'm sorry. There is nothing I can do. He did leave the Wotton Hall, the grounds and the woods around it to your stepmother."

I sagged. I couldn't understand it. He told me he would leave the house to me. He knew what it meant to me. It was my mother's dying wish for me have the house, and he promised her. I was there when he did. With tears streaming down his face he promised her. It was simply impossible that he would leave Wotton House to my stepmother when he knew very well she detested it."

"You won't be homeless," Ernest said in a comforting tone. "Your father has made provisions for you and your sister to live in the London apartment."

I could feel tears clogging my throat. My father's betrayal was impossible for me to comprehend. I was there when he drew his last breath. He held my hand and said, I love you. You are my first born and have always been my favorite. I have set it up so that you will be safe.

"I've had enough of this nonsense," Victoria, my stepmother spoke up. "Has he only left the house for me? Is there no more? What about the business? What about the ancestral jewelry, the house in Paris and Bahamas?"

Ernest cleared his throat. "I'm afraid there is nothing else for you except the house and your generous monthly allowance that will continue to be paid to you until your dying day?"

"That's it. You call that pittance a generous monthly allowance. The stingy, decrepit bastard. I had to suck his shriveled coc—"

I saw red. Without even realizing it I had jumped out of chair and was streaking across the room. The sound of my hand connecting with Victoria's cheek reverberated around our stunned figures. Victoria was holding her cheek and glaring at me with pure hatred, but she did not dare retaliate. "Get out," I snarled. "Get out. You're a vile, disrespectful bitch. Why he ever married you, I'll never know."

She smiled suddenly. "Nobody can suck like. I'm sure I could give you a lesson or two about that. You look about as frigid as a day-old corpse."

"I'm going, but let me tell you the first order of business is to sell that damn place."

She turned on her heel and left.

My sister, Lorelei came over to me. "Calm down, Scarlett. She's gone now."

I clasped my sister's hand then turned to Ernest, my voice shaking with emotion. "Can I instruct you to immediately buy the house from her?"

Ernest shook his head. "Unfortunately, no."

"Why not?"

"I'm afraid you won't be able to touch your inheritance until you are twenty-five."

Now I was genuinely confused. "What? Why would Dad make a stipulation like that?"

Ernest adjusted his glasses and shrugged. "Such stipulations are usually made when the heir is very young and might make stupid decision or be cheated by the people around that person."

"I'm not very young. I'm twenty-two. I don't make stupid decision and I don't hang around iffy people. My father knew that."

I collapsed into the chair. Was this it? I had to sit back and watch the home that has been owned by my mother's family for six hundred years be sold to strangers. I lifted my head and looked at Ernest. "There must be another way. I can't let Wotton Hall be sold to strangers. I promised my mother I would take care of it, that I would never let it go out of our family."

He looked at me from under the rims of his glasses for a moment, a strange glint in his eyes.

"There is a way, isn't there?" I pounced.

"Yes, there is, but you won't like it."

"What is it?"

He shifted in his chair and coughed discreetly. "Well, did you notice how you and your sister only hold forty-nine percent of the shares of your father's company?"

I shook my head. I had heard nothing once I knew Wotton Hall wouldn't be inherited by either my sister or me. "No, but carry on."

"That is because Zachary Black owns the other fifty one percent."

Into the fog of my rage and despair came the image of Zachary Black, a man who I didn't know what to make of. He looked like a male model and had a devilish twinkle in his eyes, but from what I'd heard from my father one shouldn't be fooled by his exterior. He was a very dangerous predator in the business of asset stripping. His job was to identify businesses that appeared vulnerable and make an aggressive takeover bid on it. "Since when?" I whispered.

"He bought the shares from your father about two years ago."

I shook my head to clear it. How strange? Why would my father sell the controlling interest of the company he had worked at all his to a man he considered a very dangerous predator? "Is the business in trouble?"

"Oh no. The business is fine. It's never been in better shape. Selling the controlling interest to Mr. Black was the best thing that you father did. The reason I mentioned him is because there is a clause in the will where if anyone jointly owns more than seventy five percent of shares they can move to stop the sale of the house, grounds and woods. Of course, you and your sister will not have enough on your own, but if you were to marry Mr. Black, you could stop the house being sold until you were old enough to buy it from your inheritance."

I stared at him with open-mouthed astonishment. "You can't be serious."

"I'm afraid I am. That is the only way for you to save Wotton Hall."

To be continued...

COME SAY HELLO!

Thank you so much for reading!
Please click on the link below to receive info about my latest
releases and giveaways.
NEVER MISS A THING

Or
come and say hello at Facebook

42145239R00113

Made in the USA
Middletown, DE
11 April 2019